THE GREY KING

THE
GREY KING

Susan Cooper

CORNERSTONE BOOKS

ABC·CLIO

Santa Barbara, California
Oxford, England

Published in Large Print by arrangement with Macmillan Publishing Company and The Bodley Head.

Cover design by CGS Studios.

ISBN 1-55736-156-8

10 9 8 7 6 5 4 3 2

This book is Smyth-sewn and printed on acid-free paper ∞ .
Manufactured in the United States of America.

for J.B. and Jacquetta

Although all the characters in this book are fictitious, the places are real. I have however taken certain liberties with the geography of the Dysynni Valley and Tal y Llyn, and there are no real farms where I have made Clwyd, Prichard's and Ty-Bont stand.

The Brenin Llwyd I did not invent.

I am grateful to the Rev. Kenneth Francis, Mr J. L. Jones and Mrs Eira Crook for kindly checking my Welsh.

On the day of the dead, when the year too
dies,
Must the youngest open the oldest hills
Through the door of the birds, where the
breeze breaks.
There fire shall fly from the raven boy,
And the silver eyes that see the wind,
And the Light shall have the harp of gold.

By the pleasant lake the Sleepers lie,
On Cadfan's Way where the kestrels call;
Though grim from the Grey King shadows
fall,
Yet singing the golden harp shall guide
To break their sleep and bid them ride.

When light from the lost land shall return,
Six Sleepers shall ride, six Signs shall burn,
And where the midsummer tree grows tall
By Pendragon's sword the Dark shall fall.

Y maent yr mynyddoedd yn canu,
ac y mae'r arglwyddes yn dod.

CONTENTS

Prologue

"Are you awake, Will? Will? Wake up, it's time for your medicine, love . . ."

The face swung like a pendulum, to and fro; rose high up in a pink blur; dropped again; divided into six pink blurs, all of them spinning madly like wheels. He closed his eyes. He could feel sweat cold on his forehead, panic cold in his mind. *I've lost it, I've forgotten!* Even in darkness the world spun round. There was a great buzzing in his head like rushing water, until for a moment the voice broke through it again.

"Will! Just for a moment, wake up . . ."

It was his mother's voice. He knew, but could not focus. The darkness whirled and roared. *I've lost something. It's gone. What is it? It was terribly important, I must remember it, I must!* He began to struggle, reaching for consciousness, and a long way off heard himself groan.

"Here we go." Another voice. The doctor. A firm arm, propping his shoulders; cold metal at his lips, a liquid tipped deftly down his throat. Automatically he swallowed. The world wildly spun. Panic came flooding again. A few faint words flashed through his mind and away like a snatch of music; his memory clutched, grasping — "*On the day of the dead —*"

Mrs Stanton stared down anxiously at the white face, the dark-smudged closed eyes, the damp hair. "What did he say?"

Suddenly Will sat upright, eyes wide and staring. "*On the day of the dead —*" He looked at her, pleading, without recognition. "That's all I can remember! It's gone! There was something I had to remember, a thing I had to do, it mattered more than anything and I've lost it! I've forgotten —" His face crumpled and he dropped back helplessly, tears running down his cheeks. His mother leaned over him, her arms round him, murmuring soothingly as if he were a baby. In a few moments he began to relax, and to breathe more easily. She looked up in distress.

"Is he delirious?"

The doctor shook his head, his round face compassionate. "No, he's past that. Physically, the worst is over. This is more like a bad dream, an hallucination — though he may indeed have lost something from his memory. The mind can be very much bound up with the health of the body, even in children ... Don't worry. He'll sleep now. And every day will be better from now on."

Mrs Stanton sighed, stroking her youngest son's damp forehead. "I'm very grateful. You've come so often — there aren't many doctors who —"

"Poof, poof," said little Dr Armstrong briskly, taking Will's wrist between finger and thumb. "We're all old friends. He was a very, very sick boy for a while. Going to be limp for a long time, too — even youngsters don't bounce back from this kind of thing very fast. I'll be back, Alice. But anyway, bed for at least another week, and no school for a month after that. Can you send him away somewhere? What about that cousin of yours in Wales, who took Mary at Easter?"

"Yes, he could go there. I'm sure he could. It's nice in October, too, and the sea air . . . I'll write to them."

Will moved his head on the pillow, muttering, but did not wake.

PART ONE

THE GOLDEN HARP

THE OLDEST HILLS

He remembered Mary had said, "They all speak Welsh, most of the time. Even Aunt Jen."

"Oh, dear," said Will.

"Don't worry," his sister said. "Sooner or later they switch to English, if they see you're there. Just remember to be patient. And they'll be extra kind because of your having been ill. At least they were to me, after my mumps."

So now Will stood patiently alone on the windy grey platform of the small station of Tywyn, in a thin drizzle of October rain, waiting while two men in the navy-blue railway uniform argued earnestly in Welsh. One of them was small and wizened, gnome-like; the other had a soft, squashy look, like a man made of dough.

The gnome caught sight of Will. "*Beth sy'n bod?*" he said.

"Er — excuse me," Will said. "My uncle said he'd meet me off the train, in the station yard, but there's no one outside. Could you tell me if there's anywhere else he might have meant?"

The gnome shook his head.

"Who's your uncle, then?" inquired the soft-faced man.

"Mr Evans, from Bryn-Crug. Clwyd Farm," Will said.

The gnome chuckled gently. "David Evans will be a bit late, boy *bach*. You have a nice dreamer for an uncle. David Evans will be late when the Last Trump sounds. You just wait a while. On holiday, is it?" Bright dark eyes peered inquisitively into his face.

"Sort of. I've had hepatitis. The doctor said I had to come away to convalesce."

"Ah!" The man nodded his head sagely. "You look a bit peaky, yes. Come to the right place, though. The air on this coast is very relaxing, they say, very relaxing. Even at this time of year."

A clattering roar came suddenly from beyond the ticket office, and through the barrier Will saw a mud-streaked Land-Rover drive into the yard. But the figure that came bounding out of it was not that of the small neat farmer he vaguely remembered; it was a wiry, gangling young man, jerkily thrusting out his hand.

"Will, is it? Hallo. Da sent me to meet you. I'm Rhys."

"How do you do." Will knew he had two grown-up Welsh cousins, old as his oldest brothers, but he had never set eyes on either of them.

Rhys scooped up his suitcase as if it had been a matchbox. "This all you have? Let's be off, then." He nodded to the railwaymen. "*Sut 'dach chi?*"

"*Iawn diolch,*" said the gnome. "Caradog Prichard was asking for you or your father, round about, this morning. Something about dogs."

"A pity you haven't seen me at all, today," Rhys said.

The gnome grinned. He took Will's ticket. "Get yourself healthy now, young man."

"Thank you," Will said.

Perched up in the front of the Land-Rover, he peered out at the little grey town as the windscreen wipers tried in vain, twitch-creak, twitch-creak, to banish the fine misty rain from the glass. Deserted shops lined the little street, and a few bent figures in raincoats scurried by; he saw a church, a small hotel, more neat houses. Then the road was widening and they were out between trim hedges, with open fields beyond, and green hills rising against the sky: a grey sky, featureless with mist. Rhys seemed shy; he drove with no attempt at talking — though the engine made so much noise that conversation would have been hard in any case. Past gaggles of silent cottages they drove, the boards that announced VACANCY or BED AND BREAKFAST swinging forlornly now that most of the holiday visitors were gone.

Rhys turned the car inland, towards the mountains, and almost at once Will had a strange new feeling of enclosure, almost of menace. The little

7

road was narrow here, like a tunnel, with its high grass banks and looming hedges like green walls on either side. Whenever they passed the gap where a hedge opened to a field through a gate, he could see the green-brown bulk of hillsides rearing up at the grey sky. And ahead, as bends in the road showed open sky briefly through the trees, a higher fold of grey hills loomed in the distance, disappearing into ragged cloud. Will felt that he was in a part of Britain like none he had ever known before: a secret, enclosed place, with powers hidden in its shrouded centuries at which he could not begin to guess. He shivered.

In the same moment, as Rhys swung round a tight corner towards a narrow bridge, the Land-Rover gave a strange jerking leap and lurched down to one side, towards the hedge. Braking hard, Rhys hauled at the wheel and managed to stop at an angle that seemed to indicate one wheel was in the ditch.

"Damn!" he said with force, opening the door.

Will scrambled after him. "What happened?"

"There is what happened." Rhys pointed a long finger at the nearside front wheel, its tyre pressed hopelessly flat against a rock jutting from the hedge. "Just look at that. Ripped it right open, and so thick those tyres are, you would never think —" His light, rather husky voice was high with astonishment.

"Was the rock lying in the road?"

Rhys shook his curly head. "Goes under the hedge. Huge, it is, that's just one end . . . I used to sit on that rock when I was half your size . . ."

Wonder had banished his shyness. "What made the car jump, then? That's the funny thing, seemed to jump, she did, right on to it, sideways. It wasn't the tyre blowing, that feels quite different . . ." He straightened, brushing away the rain that spangled his eyebrows. "Well, well. A wheel change, now."

Will said hopefully, "Can I help?"

Rhys looked down at him: at the shadowed eyes and the pale face beneath the thick, straight brown hair. He grinned suddenly, directly at Will for the first time since they had met; it made his face look quite different, untroubled and young. "Here you come down after being so ill, to be put together again, and I am to have you out in the rain changing an old wheel? Mam would have fifty fits. Back in the warm with you, go on." He moved round to the rear door of the square little car, and began pulling out tools.

Will clambered obediently up into the front of the Land-Rover again; it seemed a warm, cosy little box, after the chill wind blowing the drizzle into his face out on the road. There was no sound, there among the open fields under the looming hills, but the soft whine of the wind in telephone wires, and an occasional deep *baaa* from a distant sheep. And the rattle of a spanner; Rhys was undoing the bolts that secured the spare wheel to the back door.

Will leaned his head back against the seat, closing his eyes. His illness had kept him in bed for a long time, in a long blur of ache and distress and fleeting anxious faces, and although he had been back on his feet for more than a week, he still grew tired very easily. It was frightening sometimes to catch himself breathless and exhausted, after something as ordinary as climbing a flight of stairs.

He sat relaxed, letting the soft sounds of the wind and the calling sheep drift through his mind. Then another sound came. Opening his eyes, he saw in the side mirror another car slowing to a stop behind them.

A man climbed out, thickset, chunky, wearing a flat cap, and a raincoat flapping over rubber boots; he was grinning. For no good reason, Will instantly disliked the grin. Rhys opened the back of the Land-Rover again, to reach for the jack, and Will heard the newcomer greet him in Welsh; the words were unintelligible, but they had an unmistakable jeering tone. All this short conversation, indeed, lay as open in meaning as if Will had understood every word.

The man was clearly mocking Rhys for having to change a wheel in the rain. Rhys answered, curtly but without crossness. The man looked deliberately into the car, walking forward to peer in at the window; he stared at Will, unsmiling, with strange small light-lashed eyes, and asked Rhys something. When Rhys answered, one of the words was "Will." The man in the raincoat said something else, with a sneer in it this time directed at both of them, and then without warning he broke into an astonishing tirade of rapid, bitter speech, the words pouring out flurried and guttural like a churning river in flood. Rhys appeared to pay no attention at all. At last the man paused, angry. He swung round and marched back to his car; then he drove slowly on past them, still staring at Will as he went by. A black-and-white dog was looking out over the man's shoulder, and Will saw that the car was in fact a van, grey and windowless at the back.

He slipped across into the driver's seat and pulled open the window; the Land-Rover lurched gently up into the air beneath him as Rhys heaved on the Jack.

"Who was that?" Will said.

"Fellow called Caradog Prichard, from up the valley." Rhys spat enigmatically on his hands, and heaved again. "A farmer."

"He could have stayed and helped you."

"Ha!" Rhys said. "Caradog Prichard is not well known for helping."

"What did he say?"

"He let me know how amusing it was to see me stuck. And some things about a disagreement we have. Of no importance. And asked who you were." Rhys spun his spanner, loosening the wheel-bolts, and glanced up with a shy conspiratorial grin. "A good job our mothers were not listening, I was not polite. I said you were my cousin and none of his bloody business."

"Was he cross?"

Rhys paused reflectively. "He said — *We shall see about that.*"

Will looked up the valley road where the van had disappeared. "That's a funny thing to say."

11

"Oh," Rhys said, "that is Caradog. His hobby is to make people feel uncomfortable. Nobody likes him, except his dogs, and he doesn't even like them." He tugged at the injured wheel. "Sit still up there now. We shan't be long."

By the time he climbed back into the driving seat, rubbing his hands on an oily rag, the fine drizzle had turned to real rain; the dark hair was curling wet over his head. "Well," Rhys said. "This is nice old weather to greet you, I must say. But it won't last. We shall have a good bit of sun yet, off and on, before the winter bites down on us."

Will gazed out at the mountains, dark and distant, swinging into view as they drove along the road crossing the valley. Grey-white clouds hung ragged round the highest hills, their tops invisible behind the mist. He said, "The cloud's all tattered round the tops of the mountains. Perhaps it's breaking up."

Rhys looked out casually. "The breath of the Grey King? No, I'm sorry to tell you, Will, that's supposed to be a bad sign."

Will sat very still, a great rushing sound in his ears; he gripped the edge of his seat until the metal bit at his fingers. "What did you call it?"

"The cloud? Oh, when it hangs ragged like that we call it the breath of the *Brenin Llwyd*. The Grey King. He is supposed to live up there on the high land. It's just one of the old stories." Rhys glanced sideways at him and then braked suddenly; the Land-Rover slowed almost to a halt. "Will! Are you

12

all right? White as a ghost, you look. Are you feeling bad?"

"No. No. It was just —" Will was staring out at the grey mass of the hills. "It was just . . . the Grey King, *the Grey King* . . . it's part of something I used to know, something I was supposed to remember, for always . . . I thought I'd lost it. Perhaps — perhaps it's going to come back . . ."

Rhys crashed the car back into gear. "Oh," he called cheerfully through the noise, "we'll get you better, you just wait. Anything can happen in these old hills."

Cadfan's Way

"You see?" said Aunt Jen. "I told you it would clear up."

Will swallowed his last mouthful of bacon. "You wouldn't think it was the same country. Marvellous."

Morning sunshine streamed like banners through the windows of the long farmhouse kitchen. It glinted on the blue slate slabs of the floor, on the willow-pattern china set out on the enormous black dresser; on the shelf of beaming Toby jugs above the stove. A rainbow danced over the low ceiling, cast up in a sun-spell from the handle of the glass milk-jug.

"Warm, too," said Aunt Jen. "We are going to have an Indian summer for you, Will. And fatten you up a bit too, my dear. Have some more bread."

"It's lovely. I haven't eaten so much for months." Will watched small Aunt Jen with affection as she bustled about the kitchen. Strictly speaking, she was not his aunt at all, but a cousin of his mother's; the two had grown up as close friends, and still

14

exchanged quantities of letters. But Aunt Jen had left Buckinghamshire long before; it was one of the more romantic legends in the family, the tale of how she had come to Wales for a holiday, fallen shatteringly in love with a young Welsh farmer, and never gone home again. She even sounded Welsh herself now — and looked it, with her small, cosily plump form and bright dark eyes.

"Where's Uncle David?" he said.

"Out in the yard somewhere. This is a busy time of the year with the sheep, the hill farms send their yearlings down for the winter . . . he has to drive to Tywyn soon, he wondered if you would like to go too. Go to the beach, you could, in this sunshine."

"Super."

"No swimming, mind," said Aunt Jen hastily.

Will laughed. "I know, I'm fragile. I'll be careful . . . I'd love to go. I can send Mum a card, saying I got here in one piece." A clatter and a shadow came in the doorway; it was Rhys, dishevelled, pulling off a sweater. "Morning, Will. Have you left us some breakfast?"

"You're late," Will said cheekily.

"Late, is it?" Rhys glared at him in mock fury. "Just hear him — and us out since six with only an old cup of tea inside. Tomorrow morning, John, we will pull this young monkey out of bed and take him with us."

Behind him a deep voice chuckled. Will's attention was caught by a face he had not seen before.

15

"Will, this is John Rowlands. The best man with sheep in Wales."

"And with the harp, too," Aunt Jen said.

It was a lean face, with cheekbones carved high in it, and many lines everywhere, creased upward now round the eyes by smiling. Dark eyes, brown as coffee; thinning dark hair, streaked with grey at the sides; the well-shaped, modelled mouth of the Celt. For a moment Will stared, fascinated; there was a curious indefinable strength in this John Rowlands, even though he was not at all a big man.

"*Croeso*, Will," said John Rowlands. "Welcome to Clwyd. I heard about you from your sister, last spring."

"Good heavens," said Will in unthinking astonishment, and everyone laughed.

"Nothing bad," Rowlands said, smiling. "How is Mary?"

"She's fine," Will said. "She said she had a marvellous time here, last Easter. I was away too, then. In Cornwall."

He fell silent for a moment, his face suddenly abstracted and blank; John Rowlands looked at him swiftly, then sat down at the table where Rhys was already poised over bacon and eggs. Will's uncle came in, carrying a batch of papers.

"*Cwpanaid o de, cariad?*" said Aunt Jen, when she saw him.

"*Diolch yn fawr,*" said David Evans, taking the cup of tea she held out to him. "And then I must be off to Tywyn. You want to come, Will?"

"Yes, please."

"We may be a couple of hours." The sound of his words was very precise always; he was a small, neatly-made man, sharp-featured, but with an unexpectedly vague, reflective look sometimes in his dark eyes. "I have to go to the bank, and to see Llew Thomas, and there will be the new tyre for the Land-Rover. The car that jumped up in the air and got itself a puncture."

Rhys, with his mouth full, made a strangled noise of protest. "Now, Da," he said, swallowing. "I know how it sounded, but really I am not mad, there was *nothing* that could have made her swerve over to the side like that and hit the rock. Unless the steering rod is going."

"There is nothing wrong with the steering of that car," David Evans said.

"Well, then!" Rhys was all elbows and indignation. "I tell you she just lurched over for no reason at all. Ask Will."

"It's true," Will said. "The car did just sort of jump sideways and hit that rock. I don't see what could have made it jump, unless it had run over a loose stone in the road — but that would have had to be a pretty big stone. And there was no sign of one anywhere."

"Great allies, you two, already, I can see," said his uncle. He drained his teacup, gazing at them over the top; Will was not sure whether or not he was laughing at them. "Well, well, I will have the

17

steering checked anyway. John, Rhys, now that extra fencing for the *fridd* —"

They slid into Welsh, unthinking. It did not bother Will. He was occupied in trying to scorn away a small voice at the back of his mind, an irrational small voice with an irrational suggestion. *"If they want to know what made the car jump,"* this part of his mind was whispering at him, *"why don't they ask Caradog Prichard?"*

David Evans dropped Will at a small newsagent's shop, where he could buy postcards, and chugged off to leave the Land-Rover at a garage. Will bought a card showing a sinister dark lake surrounded by very Welsh-looking mountains, wrote on it "I GOT HERE! Everyone sends their love," and sent it off to his mother from the Post Office, a solemn and unmistakable red brick building on a corner of Tywyn High Street. Then he looked about him, wondering where to go next.

Choosing at random, hoping to see the sea, he turned right up the narrow curving High Street. Before long he found that there would be no sea this way: nor anything but shops, houses, a cinema with an imposing Victorian front grandly labelled ASSEMBLY ROOMS, and the slate-roofed lych-gate of church.

Will liked investigating churches; before his illness had overtaken him, he and two friends from school had been cycling all round the Thames Valley to make brass rubbings. He turned into the little churchyard, to see if there might be any brasses here.

The church porch was low-roofed, deep as a cave; inside, the church was shadowy and cool, with sturdy white painted walls and massive white pillars. Nobody was there. Will found no brasses for rubbing, but only monuments to unpronounceable benefactors, like Gruffydd ap Adda of Ynysymaengwyn Hall. At the rear of the church, on his way out, he noticed a strange long grey stone set up on end, incised with marks too ancient for him to decipher. He stared at it for a long moment; it seemed like an omen of some kind, though of what significance he had not the least idea. And then, in the porch on his way out, he glanced idly up at the notice-board with its scattering of parish news, and he saw the name: *Church of St Cadfan.*

The whirling came again in his ears like the wind; staggering, he collapsed on to the low bench in the porch. His mind spun, he was back suddenly in the roaring confusion of his illness, when he had known that something, something most precious, had slipped or been taken away from his memory. Words flickered through his consciousness, without order or meaning, and then a phrase surfaced like a leaping fish: *"On Cadfan's Way where the kestrels call. . . ."* His mind seized it greedily, reaching for more. But there was no more. The roaring died away; Will opened his eyes, breathing more steadily, the giddiness draining gradually out of him. He said softly, aloud, "On Cadfan's Way where the kestrels

19

call ... On Cadfan's Way ..." Outside in the sun-shine the grey slate tombstones and green grass glimmered, with jewel-glints of light here and there from droplets of rain still clinging to the longest stems from the day before. Will thought, *"On the day of the dead ... the Grey King ... there must have been some sort of warning about the Grey King ... and what is Cadfan's Way?"*

"Oh," he said aloud in sudden fury, "if only I could *remember!*"

He jumped up and went back to the newsagent's shop. "Please," he said, "is there a guide to the church, or to the town?"

"Nothing on Tywyn," said the red-cheeked girl of the shop, in her sibilant Welsh lilt. "Too late in the season, you are ... but Mr Owen has a leaflet for sale in the church, I think. And there is this, if you like. Full of lovely walks." She showed him a *Guide to North Wales*, for thirty-five pence.

"Well," said Will, counting out his money rather reluctantly. "I can always take it home afterwards, I suppose."

"It would make a very nice present," said the girl earnestly. "Got some beautiful pictures, it has. And just look at the cover!"

"Thank you," said Will.

When he peered at the little book, outside, it told him that the Saxons had settled in Tywyn in A.D. 516, round the church built by St Cadfan of Brittany and his holy well, and that the inscribed stone in the church was said to be the oldest piece of written

20

Welsh in existence, and could be translated: "The body of Cyngen is on the side between where the marks will be. In the retreat beneath the mound is extended Cadfan, said that it should enclose the praise of the earth. May he rest without blemish." But it said not a word about Cadfan's Way. Nor, when he checked, did the leaflet in the church.

Will thought: it is not Cadfan I want, it is his Way. A way is a road. A way where the kestrels call must be a road over a moor, or a mountain.

It pushed even the seashore out of his mind, when later he walked absentmindedly for a while among the breakwaters of the windy beach. When he met his uncle for the ride back to the farm, he found no help there either.

"Cadfan's Way?" said David Evans. "You pronounce it Cadvan, by the way; one *f* is always a *v* sound in Welsh . . . Cadfan's Way . . . No. It does sound a bit familiar, you know. But I couldn't tell you, Will. John Rowlands is the one to ask about things like that. He has a mind like an encyclopedia, does John, full of old things."

John Rowlands was out somewhere on the farm, busy, so for the time being Will had to content himself with a much-folded map. He went out with it that afternoon, alone in the sunlit valley, to walk the boundaries of the farm; his uncle had roughly pencilled them in for him. Clwyd was a lowland farm, stretching across most of the valley of the Dysynni River; some of its land was marshy, near the river, and some stretched up the soaring scree-patched side of the mountain, green and grey and bracken-brown. But most was lush green valley land, fertile and friendly, part of it left new-ploughed since the harvest of this year's crops, and all the rest serving as pasture for square, sturdy Welsh Black cattle. On the mountain land, only sheep grazed. Some of the lower slopes had been ploughed, though even they looked so steep to Will that he wondered how a tractor ploughing them could have kept from rolling over. Above those, nothing grew but bracken, groups of wind-warped scrubby trees, and grass; the mountain reared up to the sky, and the deep aimless call of a sheep came now and then floating down into the still, warm afternoon.

It was by another sound that he found John Rowlands, unexpectedly. As he was walking through one of the Clwyd fields towards the river, with a high wild hedge on one side of him and the dark ploughed soil on the other, he heard a dull, muffled thudding, somewhere ahead. Then suddenly at a curve in the field he saw the figure, moving steadily and rhythmically as if in a slow, deliberate dance. He stopped and watched, fascinated. Rowlands, his shirt half-open and a red kerchief tied round his neck, was making a transformation. He moved gradually along the hedge, first chopping carefully here and there with a murderous tool like a cross between an axe and a pirate's cutlass, then setting this down and hauling and interweaving whatever remained of the long, rank growth. Before him, the hedge grew wild and high, great arms groping out uncontrolled in all directions as the hazel and hawthorn did their best to grow into full-fledged trees. Behind him, as he moved along his relentless swaying way, he left instead a neat fence: scores of beheaded branches bristling waist-high like spears, with every fifth branch bent mercilessly down at right angles and woven in along the rest as if it were part of a hurdle.

Will watched, silent, until Rowlands became aware of him and straightened up, breathing heavily. He pulled the red kerchief loose, wiped his forehead with it and re-tied it loosely round his neck. In his creased brown face, the lines beside the dark eyes turned upwards just a little as he looked at Will.

"I know," he said, the velvet voice solemn. "You are thinking, here is this wonderful healthy hedge full of leaves and hawthorn berries, reaching up to the heavens, and here is this man hacking it down like a butcher jointing a sheep, taming it into a horrid little naked fence, all bones and no grace."

Will grinned. "Well," he said. "Something like that, yes."

"Ah," said John Rowlands. He squatted down on his haunches, resting his axe head down on the ground between his knees and leaning on it. "*Duw*, it's a good job you came along. I cannot go so fast as I used to. Well, let me tell you now, if we were to leave this lovely wild hedge the way it is now, and has been for too long, it would take over half the field before this time next year. And even though I am cutting off its head and half its body, all these sad bent-over shoots that you see will be sending up so many new arms next spring that you will hardly notice any difference in it at all."

"Now that you come to mention it," said Will, "yes, of course, the hedging is just the same at home, in Bucks. It's just that I never actually watched anyone doing it before."

"Had my eye on this hedge for a year," John Rowlands said. "It was missed last winter. Like life it is, Will — sometimes you must seem to hurt something in order to do good for it. But not often a very big hurt, thank goodness." He got to his feet again. "You look more healthy already, *bachgen*. The Welsh sun is good for you."

Will looked down at the map in his hand. "Mr Rowlands," he said, "can you tell me anything about Cadfan's Way?"

The Welshman had been running one tough brown finger along the edge of his mattock; there was a second's pause in the movement, and then the finger moved on. He said quietly, "Now what put that into your head, I wonder?"

"I don't really know. I suppose I must have read it somewhere. Is there a Cadfan's Way?"

"Oh, yes, indeed," John Rowlands said. "*Llwybr Cadfan*. No secret about that, though most people these days have forgotten it. I think they have a Cadfan Road in one of the new Tywyn housing estates instead ... St Cadfan was a kind of missionary, from France, in the days when Brittany and Cornwall and Wales all had close ties. Fourteen hundred years ago he had his church in Tywyn, and a holy well — and he is supposed to have founded the monastery on *Enlli*, that is in English Bardsey, as well. You know Bardsey Island, where the bird-watchers go, out there off the tip of North Wales? People used to visit Tywyn and go on to Bardsey — and so, they say, there is an old pilgrims' road that goes over the mountain from Machynlleth to Tywyn, past Abergynolwyn. And along the side of this valley, no doubt. Or perhaps higher up. Most of the old ways go along high places, they were safer there. But nobody knows where to find Cadfan's Way now."

"I see," said Will. It was more than enough; he knew that now he would be able to find the Way, given time. But increasingly he felt that there was very little time left; that it was urgent for his quest, so oddly lost by his memory, to be accomplished very soon. *On the day of the dead.* . . . And what was the quest, and where, and why? If only he could remember . . .

John Rowlands turned towards the hedge again. "Well —"

"I'll see you later," Will said. "Thank you. I'm trying to walk all round the edge of the farm."

"Take it gently. That is a long walk for a convalescent, the whole of it." Rowlands straightened suddenly, pointing a finger at him in warning. "And if you go up the valley and get to the Craig yr Aderyn end — that way — make sure you check the boundaries on your map, and do not go off

25

your uncle's land. That is Caradog Prichard's farm beyond, and he is not kind with trespassers."

Will thought of the malicious, light-lashed eyes in the sneering face he had seen from the Land-Rover with Rhys.

"Oh," he said. "Caradog Prichard. All right. Thanks. *Diolch yn fawr.* Is that right?"

John Rowlands's face broke into creases of laughter. "Not bad," he said. "But perhaps you should stick to just *diolch.*"

The gentle thud of his axe dwindled behind Will and was lost in the insect-hum of the sunny afternoon, with the scattered calls of birds and sheep. The way that Will was going led sideways across the valley, with the grey-green sweep of the mountain rising always before him; it blocked out more and more of the sky as he walked on. Soon he was beginning to climb, and then the bracken began to come in over the grass in a rustling knee-high carpet, with clumps here and there of spiky green gorse, its yellow flowers still bright among the fierce prickling stalks. No hedge climbed the mountain, but a slate-topped drystone wall, curving with every contour, broken now and then by a stile-step low enough for men but too high for sheep.

Will found himself losing breath far more quickly than he would normally have done. As soon as he next came to a humped rock the right size for sitting, he folded thankfully into a panting heap. While he waited for his breath to come properly back, he looked at the map again. The Clwyd farmland seemed to end about halfway up the mountain — but there was, of course, nothing to guarantee that he would come across the old Cadfan's Way before he reached the boundary. He found himself hoping a little nervously that the rest of the mountain above was not Caradog Prichard's land.

Stuffing the map back into his pocket, he went on, higher, through the crackling brown fronds of the bracken. He was climbing diagonally now, as the slope grew steeper. Birds whirred away from him; somewhere high above, a skylark was pouring out its rippling, throbbing song. Then all at once, Will began to have an unaccountable feeling that he was being followed.

Abruptly he stopped, swinging round. Nothing moved. The bracken-brown slope lay still beneath the sunshine, with outcrops of white rock glimmering here and there. A car hummed past on the road below, invisible through trees; he was high above the farm now, looking out over the silver thread of the river to the mountains rising green and grey and brown behind, and at last fading blue into the distance. Further up the valley the mountainside on which he stood was clothed dark green with plantations of spruce trees, and beyond those he could see a great grey-black crag rising, a lone peak, lower than the mountains around it yet dominating all the surrounding land. A few large black birds circled its top; as he watched, they merged together into a shape of a long V, as geese do, and flew unhurriedly away over the mountain in the direction of the sea.

Then from somewhere close, he heard one short sharp bark from a dog.

Will jumped. No dog was likely to be on the mountain alone. Yet there was no sign of another human being anywhere. If someone was near by, why was he hiding himself?

He turned to go on up the slope, and only then did he see the dog. He stood stone-still. It was poised directly above him, alert, waiting; a white dog, white all over with only one small black patch on its back, like a saddle. Except for the curious pattern of colouring, it looked like a traditional Welsh sheep dog, muscular and sharp-muzzled, with feathered legs and tail: a smaller version of the collie. Will held out his hand. "Here, boy," he said. But the dog bared its teeth, and gave a low, threatening growl deep in its throat.

Will took a few tentative steps up the slope, diagonally, in the direction he had been going before. Crouching on its stomach, the dog moved with him, teeth glittering, tongue lolling. The attitude was odd and yet familiar, and suddenly Will realized that he had seen it the evening before in the two dogs on his uncle's farm that had been helping Rhys bring in the cows to be milked. It was the movement of control — the watchful crouch from which a working sheepdog would spring, to bring to order the animals it was driving in a particular direction.

But where was this dog trying to drive him?

Clearly, there was only one way to find out. Taking a deep breath, Will turned to face the dog and began deliberately clambering straight up the slope. The dog stopped, and the long, low growl began again in its throat; it crouched, back curved as if all four feet were planted like trees in the ground. The snarl of the white teeth said, very plainly: *Not this way.* But Will, clenching his fists, kept climbing. He shifted direction very slightly so that he would pass close to the dog without touching it. But then unexpectedly, with one short bark, the dog darted towards him, crouching low, and involuntarily Will jumped — and lost his balance. He fell sideways on the steep hillside. Desperately reaching his arms wide to stop himself from rolling headlong down, he slithered and bumped upside-down for a few wild yards, terror loud as a shout in his head, until his fall was checked by something jerking fiercely at his sleeve. He came up against a rock, with a numbing thud.

He opened his eyes. The line where mountain met sky was spinning before him. Very close was the dog, its teeth clamped on the sleeve of his jacket, tugging him back, all warm breath and black nose and staring eyes. And at the sight of the eyes, Will's world spun round and over again so fast that he thought he must still be falling. The roaring was in his ears again, and all things normal became suddenly chaos. For this dog's eyes were like no eyes he had ever seen; where they should have been

29

brown, they were silver white: eyes the colour of blindness, set in the head of an animal that could see. And as the silver eyes gazed into his, and the dog's breath panted out hot on his face, in a whirling instant Will remembered everything that his illness had taken away from him. He remembered the verses that had been put into his head as guide for the bleak, lone quest he was destined now to follow; remembered who he was and what he was — and recognized the design that under the mask of coincidence had brought him here to Wales.

At the same time another kind of innocence fell away, and he was aware too of immense danger, like a great shadow across the world, waiting for him all through this unfamiliar land of green valleys and dark-misted mountain peaks. He was like a battle leader suddenly given news: suddenly made aware, as he had not been a moment before, that just beyond the horizon a great and dreadful army lay in wait, preparing itself to rise like a huge wave and drown all those who stood in its way.

Trembling with wonder, Will reached across his other arm and fondled the dog's ears. It let go of his sleeve and stood there gazing at him, tongue lolling pink from a pink-rimmed mouth.

"Good dog," Will said. "Good dog." Then a dark figure blotted out the sun, and he rolled abruptly over to sit up and see who stood outlined there against the sky.

A clear Welsh voice said: "Are you hurt?"

It was a boy. He was dressed neatly in what looked like a school uniform: grey trousers, white shirt, red socks and tie. He had a schoolbag slung over one shoulder, and he seemed to be about the same age as Will. But there was a quality of strangeness about him, as there had been about the dog, that tightened Will's throat and caught him motionless in a wondering stare; for this boy was drained of all colour, like a shell bleached by the summer sun. His hair was white, and his eyebrows. His skin was pale. The effect was so startling that for a wild moment Will found himself wondering whether the hair was deliberately bleached — done on purpose, to create astonishment and alarm. But the idea vanished as swiftly as it had come. The mixture of arrogance and hostility facing him showed plainly that this was not that kind of boy at all.

"I'm all right." Will stood up, shaking, pulling bits of bracken out of his hair and off his clothes. He said, "You might teach your dog the difference between people and sheep."

"Oh," said the boy indifferently, "he knew what he was about. He would have done you no harm." He said something to the dog in Welsh, and it trotted back up the hill and sat down beside him, watching them both.

"Well" — Will began, and then he stopped. He had looked into the boy's face and found there another pair of eyes to shake him off balance. It was not, this time, the unearthliness he had seen in the dog; it was a sudden shock of feeling that he had

31

seen them somewhere before. The boy's eyes were a strange, tawny golden colour like the eyes of a cat or a bird, rimmed with eyelashes so pale as to be almost invisible, they had a cold, unfathomable glitter.

"*The raven boy*," he said instantly. "That's who you are, that's what it calls you, the old verse. I have it all now, I can remember. But ravens are black. Why does it call you that?"

"My name is Bran," the boy said, unsmiling, looking unwinking down at him. "Bran Davies. I live down on your uncle's farm."

Will was taken aback for a moment, in spite of his new confidence. "On the farm?"

"With my father. In a cottage. My father works for David Evans." He blinked in the sunshine, pulled a pair of sunglasses from his pocket, and put them on; the tawny eyes disappeared into shadow. He said, in exactly the same conversational tone, "Bran is really the Welsh word for crow. But people called Bran in the old stories are linked up with the raven, too. A lot of ravens in these hills, there are. So I suppose you could say 'the raven boy' if you wanted. Poetic licence, like."

He swung the satchel off his shoulder and sat down beside Will on a rock, fiddling with the leather strap.

Will said, "How did you know who I was? That David Evans is my uncle?"

"I could just as well ask how you knew me," Bran said. "How did you know, to name me the raven boy?"

He ran one finger idly up and down the strap. Then he smiled suddenly, a smile that illuminated his pale face like quick flaring fire, and he pulled off the dark glasses again.

"I will tell you the answer to both questions, Will Stanton," he said. "It is because you are not properly human, but one of the Old Ones of the Light put here to hold back the terrible power of the Dark. You are the last of that circle to be born on earth. And I have been waiting for you."

The Raven Boy

"You see," Will said, "it's the first quest, without help, for me — and the last, because this now is the raising of the last defence the Light can build, to be ready. There is a great battle ahead, Bran — not yet, but not far off. For the Dark is rising, to make its great attempt to take the world for itself until the end of time. When that happens, we must fight and we must win. But we can only win if we have the right weapons. That is what we have been doing, and are still, in such quests as this — gathering the weapons forged for us long, long ago. Six enchanted Signs of the Light, a golden grail, a wonderful harp, a crystal sword . . . They are all achieved now but the harp and the sword, and I do not know what will be the manner of the sword's finding. But the quest for the harp is mine . . ."

He picked a sprig of gorse, and sat staring at it. "Out of a long time ago, there were three verses made," he said, "to tell me what to do. They aren't written down any more, though once they were. They are only in my mind. Or at least they used to be — forever, I thought. But then not long ago I was very ill, and when I came out of it, the verses had gone. I'd forgotten them. I don't know if the Dark had a hand in it. That's possible, while I was . . . not myself. They couldn't have taken the words for themselves, but they could have managed to hinder my catching them again. I thought I'd go mad, trying to remember. I didn't know what to do. A few bits came back, but not much . . . not much. Until I saw your dog."

"Cafall," Bran said. The dog raised its head.

"Cafall. Those eyes of his, those silver eyes . . . it was as if they broke a spell. He had put me on the Old Way, Cadfan's Way, as well — just here. And I remembered. All the verses. Everything."

"He is a special dog," Bran said. "He is not . . . ordinary. What are your verses?"

Will looked at him, opened his mouth, shut it again, and looked out at the mountains in confusion. The white-haired boy laughed. He said, "I know. For all you can tell, I might be from the Dark in spite of Cafall. Isn't that it?"

Will shook his head. "If you were from the Dark, I should know very well. There's a sense, that tells us . . . the trouble is, that same particular sense that says you aren't from the Dark doesn't say anything else about you either. Not a thing. Nothing bad, nothing good. I don't understand."

"Ah," Bran said mockingly. "I have never understood that myself. But I can tell you, I am like Cafall — I am not quite ordinary either." He glanced at

Will, the pale-lashed eyes darting, secretive. Then he said, reciting deliberately, sounding very sing-song Welsh:

"On the day of the dead, when the year too dies,
Must the youngest open the oldest hills
Through the door of the birds, where the breeze breaks."

Will sat stone-still, horrified, gazing at him. The land broke in waves. The sky was falling. He said huskily, "The beginning of it. But you can't know that. It's not possible. There are only three people in the world who —"

He stopped.

The white-haired boy said, "I was up here with Cafall, a week ago, up here where you never meet anybody, and we met an old man. A strange old man he was, with a lot of white hair and a big beaky nose."

Will said slowly, "Ah."

"He was not English," said Bran, "and he was not Welsh either, though he spoke good Welsh, and good English too, for that matter . . . He must have been a *dewin*, a wizard, he knew a lot about me . . ." He pulled a frond of bracken, frowning, and began to pick it to pieces. "A lot about me . . . Then he told me about the Dark and the Light. I have never heard anything that I believed so very much, right away, without question. And he told me about you. He told me that it was my task to help you on your quest, but that" — a mocking note slid again into the clear voice, perceptible just for an instant —

"but that because you would not trust me, I must learn those three lines, for a sign. And so he taught me them."

Will lifted his head to look up the valley, at the blue-grey hills hazy in the sunshine and he shivered; the sense of a looming shadow was on him again, like a dark cloud hovering. Then he said, shrugging it aside, speaking without strain of suspicion now, "There are three verses. But the first two are the ones that matter, for now. The lines my master Merriman taught you come at the beginning.

"On the day of the dead, when the year too dies,
Must the youngest open the oldest hills
Through the door of the birds, where the breeze breaks.
There fire shall fly from the raven boy,
And the silver eyes that see the wind,
And the Light shall have the harp of gold.

"By the pleasant lake the Sleepers lie,
On Cadfan's Way where the kestrels call;
Though grim from the Grey King shadows fall,
Yet singing the golden harp shall guide
To break their sleep and bid them ride."

He reached out and rubbed Cafall's ears. "The silver eyes," he said. There was a silence, with only the distant skylark still trilling faintly in the air. Bran had listened without moving, his pale face intent. At length he said, "Who is Merriman?"

"The old man you met, of course. If you mean, what is he, that's harder. Merriman is my master. He is the first of the Old Ones, and the strongest, and the wisest . . . He will have no part in this quest now, I think. Not in the seeking. There are too many things for all of us to do, in too many places."

"Cadfan's Way, it said in the verse. I remember he told me one other thing, he said Cafall would get you on to the Way, so that the two things together, the place and Cafall himself, would be important — then he said, *and also the Way for later.* Later — so not yet, I suppose." Bran sighed. "What does it all mean?" For all his strangeness, it was the plaintive question of a very normal boy.

"I was thinking," Will said, "that the day of the dead might be All Hallows' Eve. Don't you think? Hallowe'en, when people used to believe all the ghosts walked."

"I know some who still believe they do," Bran said. "Things like that last a long time, up here. There is one old lady I know puts out food for the spirits, at Hallowe'en. She says they eat it too, though if you ask me it is more likely the cats, she has four of them . . . Hallowe'en will be this next Saturday, you know."

"Yes," Will said. "I do know. Very close."

"Some people say that if you go and sit in the church porch till midnight on Hallowe'en, you hear a voice calling out the names of everyone who will die in the next year," Bran grinned. "I have never tried it."

But Will was not smiling as he listened. He said thoughtfully, "You just said, *in the next year.* And the verse says, 'On the day of the dead *when the*

38

year too dies.' But that doesn't make sense. Hallowe'en isn't the end of the year."

"Maybe once upon a time it used to be," Bran said. "The end and the beginning both, once, instead of December. In Welsh, Hallowe'en is called *Calan Gaeaf,* and that means the first day of winter. Pretty warm for winter, of course. Mind you, nobody is going to get me to spend the night in St Cadfan's churchyard, however warm."

"I was there this morning, at St Cadfan's," Will said. "That was what put the name back into my head, somehow, to come and look for the Way. But now I have the verse, I must begin at the beginning."

"The hardest part," Bran said. He tugged off his school tie, rolled it up and stuffed it into his trouser pocket. "It says, *the youngest must open the oldest hills, through the door of the birds.* Right? And you are the youngest of the Old Ones, and these are the oldest hills in Britain for sure, these and the Scottish hills. But the door of the birds, that's hard ... The birds have their holes and nests everywhere, the mountains are full of birds. Crows, kestrels, ravens, buzzards, plovers, wrens, wheatears, pipits, curlews — lovely it is, listening to the curlews down on the marshes in spring. And look, there is a peregrine." He pointed upwards, to a dark speck in the clear blue sky drifting lazily round in a great sweeping curve, far above their heads.

"How can you tell?"

"A kestrel would be smaller, so would a merlin. It isn't a crow. It could be a buzzard. But I think it's a peregrine — you get to know them, they are so scarce now that you look more carefully . . . and I have a reason of my own too, because peregrines like to bother ravens, and as you pointed out, I am the raven boy."

Will studied him: the eyes were hidden again behind the sunglasses, and the pale face, almost as pale as the hair, was expressionless. It must always be difficult to read this boy Bran; to know properly what he was thinking or feeling. Yet here he was, part of the pattern: found by Merriman, Will's master, and now by Will — and described in a prophetic verse that had been made more than a thousand years ago . . .

He said, experimentally, "Bran."

"What?"

"Nothing. I was just practising. It's a funny name, I never heard it before."

"The only way it is funny is in that English voice of yours. It is not bran like a breakfast cereal, it is longer-sounding, *braaan, braaan.*"

"*Braaaaaaan,*" said Will.

"Better." He squinted at Will over the top of the sunglasses. "Is that a map sticking out of your pocket? Let's have it here a minute."

Will handed it over. Squatting on the hillside, Bran spread it on the rustling bracken. "Now," he said. "Read out the names that I point to."

Will peered obediently at the moving finger. He saw: Tal y Llyn, Mynydd Ceiswyn, Cemmaes, Llanwrin, Machynlleth, Afon Dyfi, Llangelynin. He read aloud, laboriously, "Tallylin, Minid Seeswin, Semeyes, Lan-rin Machine-leth, Affon Diffy, Lang-elly-nin."

Bran moaned softly. "I was afraid of that."

"Well," said Will defensively, "that's exactly what they look like. Oh, wait a minute, I remember Uncle David said you pronounce *f* like *v*. So that makes this one 'Avon Divvy.' "

"Duvvy," said Bran. "Written in English, Dovey. The Afon Dyfi is the River Dovey, and that place over there is called Aberdyfi, which means the mouth of the Dovey, Aberdovey. The Welsh *y* is mostly like the English u in 'run' or 'hunt.' "

"Mostly?" said Will suspiciously.

"Well, sometimes it isn't. But you'd better stick to that for now. Look here —" He fumbled inside his leather satchel and brought out a school note-book and pencil. He wrote: Mynydd Ceiswyn. "Now that," he said, "is pronounced *Munuth Kice-ooin. Kice* like *rice*. Go on, say it."

Will said it, peering incredulously at the spelling.

"Three things there," said Bran, writing. He appeared to be enjoying himself. "Double *d* is always a 'th' sound, but a soft sound, like in 'leather', not in 'smith.' Then, *c* is always a hard sound in Welsh, like in 'cat'. So is *g*, as a matter of fact — it's always *g* as in 'go', not *g* as in 'gentle'. And the Welsh *w* is like the *oo* sound in 'pool', nearly always. So that's why Mynydd Ceiswyn is pronounced Munuth Kice-oo-in."

Will said, "But it ought to be *un* at the end, not *in*, because you said the Welsh *y* was like *u* in 'run'."

Bran chuckled. "There's a memory. Sorry. That's one of the times when it isn't. You'll just have to get used to them if you're going to say the places right. After all you can't complain about us not being consistent, not when your old English is full of things like dough and through and thorough."

Will took the pencil and copied from the map "Cemmaes" and "Llangelynin." "All right then," he said. "If the *c* is hard, then it must be *Kem-eyes*."

"Very good," Bran said. "But a hard *s*, not soft. Said fast it comes out *Kemmess*. Like chemist, without the *t*."

Will sighed, looking hard at his next sample, "Hard *g*, and the *y* sound. So it's . . . *Lan-gel-un-in*."

"You're getting there," Bran said. "All you have to learn now is the one sound most Englishmen can never manage. Open your mouth a little way and put the tip of your tongue against the back of your front teeth. As if you're just about to say *lan*."

Will gave him a doubtful look, but did what he was told. Then he twitched his lips upwards, and made a face like a rabbit.

"Stop it," said Bran, spluttering. "Get educated, man. Now while your tongue is there, blow round the sides of it. Both sides at once."

Will blew.

"That's right. Now, say the word *lan* but give a bit of a blow before you bring it out. Like this: *llan, llan.*"

"Llan, llan," said Will, feeling like a steam engine, and stopped in astonishment. "Hey, that sounds Welsh!"

"Pretty good," said Bran critically. "You'll have to practise. Actually when a Welshman says it, his tongue isn't like that and the whole sound comes out from the sides of his mouth, but that's no good for a *Sais*. You'll do all right. And if you get fed up with trying, you can take the other English way out and say *ll* like *thl*."

"Enough," said Will. "Enough."

"Just try one more," Bran said. "You wouldn't believe the way some people say this one. Well, yes you would, because you did too." He wrote: Machynlleth.

Will groaned, and took a deep breath. "Well — there's the *y* — and the *ll* —"

"And the *ch* is sort of breathy, the way the Scots say *loch*. At the back of your throat, like."

"Why do you people make everything so complicated? Mach . . . un . . . lleth."

"Machynlleth."

"Machynlleth."

"Not bad at all."

"But mine doesn't really sound like yours. Yours sounds wetter. Like German. *Achtung! Achtung!*" Will yelled suddenly at the top of his voice, and Cafall jumped up and barked, tail waving.

"Do you speak German?"

"Good Lord, no! I heard that in some old film. *Achtung!* Machynlleth!"

"*Machynlleth*," said Bran.

"You see, yours does sound wetter. Sploshier. I expect all Welsh babies dribble a lot."

"Get out of here," said Bran, and grabbed at him as Will dodged away. They ran down the mountain, laughing, in a wild zigzag, with Cafall bounding joyously alongside.

But halfway, Will stumbled and slowed down; without warning, he felt giddy, his legs weak and unreliable. He staggered to a near-by wall and leaned against it, panting. Bran yelled cheerfully over his shoulder as he ran, satchel flying; then slowed, stopped, looked more carefully and came back.

"Are you all right, then?"

"I think so. Head hurts. It's my stupid legs though, they give out too easily. I suppose I'm still getting better, really — I was ill, for a while —"

"I knew, and I ought to have remembered." Bran stood fidgeting, cross with himself. "Your friend Mr Merriman said you'd been even more ill than anyone realized."

"But he wasn't there," Will said. "Well. Not that that means a thing, of course."

"Sit down," Bran said. "Put your head down on your knees."

"I'm okay. Really. Just have to get my breath back."

"We're very close to home, or we should be. Just a few hundred yards over that way —" Bran scrambled up on the high dry stone wall to give himself a better view.

But while he stood there, suddenly a great angry yell came from the other side of the wall, and the barking of dogs. Will saw Bran draw himself up tall and straight where he stood on the wall, looking down haughtily. He heaved himself upright to peep over the slate-topped edge, past Bran's feet, and saw a man approaching at a half-run, shouting, and waving one arm angrily; in the other arm he carried what looked like a shotgun. When he came closer, he began calling to Bran in Welsh. Will did not recognize him at first, for he wore no hat, and the tousled head of raw red hair was unfamiliar. Then he saw that it was Caradog Prichard.

When the farmer paused for breath, Bran said clearly, pointedly using English, "My dog does not chase sheep, Mr Prichard. And anyway he is not on your land, he is over this side of the wall."

"I tell you that he is a rogue dog, and he has been worrying my sheep!" Prichard said furiously; his English was sibilant, heavily accented, thickened by rage. "Him and that damn black hound of John Rowlands. I will shoot them both if I catch them at it, you be sure I will. And you and your little English friend there had better keep off my land too, if you know what's good for you." The small eyes in his flushed, pudgy face glared maliciously at Will.

Will said nothing. Bran did not move; he stood there looking down at the angry farmer. He said softly, "Bad luck you would have, if you shot Cafall, Caradog Prichard." He ran one hand through his white hair, pushing it back, in a gesture that seemed to Will oddly affected. "You want to look more closely at those sheep," Bran said, "before you go blaming dogs for what is foxes' work."

"Foxes!" said Prichard contemptuously. "I know a fox's killing when I see it, and I know a rogue dog too. Keep away from my land, both of you." But he was not meeting Bran's eye now, nor looking at Will; he swung round without another word and strode off across the pasture, with his dogs trotting at his heels.

Bran climbed down from the wall.

"Bah!" he said. "Worrying sheep! Cafall is a match for any working dog in this valley; he would never in the world go wild after any sheep, let alone on Caradog Prichard's land." He looked at the vanishing Prichard, and then at Will, and smiled. It was a strange sly smile; Will was not sure that he liked it.

"You will find out," Bran said, "that people like him are a bit afraid of me, deep down. It is because I am albino, you see. The white hair, and funny eyes, and not much pigment in the skin — a bit of a freak, you might say."

"I shouldn't," Will said mildly.

"Maybe not," Bran said without much belief, acid in his tongue. "But it is said often enough at school

... and outside too, by nice men like Mr Prichard. You see, all good Welshmen are dark, dark of hair and dark of eyes, and the only fair-skinned creatures in Wales, in the old days, were the *Tylwyth Teg*. The old spirits, the little people. Anyone as fair as me must have something to do with the *Tylwyth Teg*. . . . Nobody believes in such things any more, oh no, of course not, but in the middle of the winter night when the wind is blowing dark and the old television is not on, I bet you half the people in this valley would not like to swear that I could not bring the Evil Eye on them."

Will scratched his head. "There was certainly something . . . fidgety . . . in the way that man looked at you, when you said —" He shook his shoulders, like a dog coming out of water. He did not look at Bran; he disliked the shadows of crafty arrogance that this talking had put over the other boy's face. It was a pity, it shouldn't be necessary; one day he would take it away . . . He said, "Caradog Prichard isn't dark. He has red hair. Like carrots."

"His family is from Dinas Mawddwy way," Bran said. "His mother, anyway. There was supposed to be a whole tribe of villains up there once, all red-haired, real terrors. Anyway there are still redheads come from Dinas today."

"Would he really shoot Cafall?"

"Yes," Bran said shortly. "Caradog Prichard is very strange. There is a saying that anyone who spends the night alone up on Cader will come down next morning either a poet, or mad. And my father says that once when he was young, Caradog Prichard did spend the night alone up on Cader, because he wanted to be a great bard.''

"It can't have worked."

"Well. Perhaps it worked in one way. He is not much of a poet, but he often acts as if he were more than a little bit mad."

"What is Cader?"

Bran stared at him. "Don't know much about Wales, do you? Cader Idris, over there." He pointed to the line of blue grey peaks across the valley. "One of the highest mountains in Wales. You should know about Cader. After all it comes in your verse."

Will frowned. "No, it doesn't."

"Oh, yes. Not by name, no — but it's important in that second part. That's where he lives you see, up on Cader. The Brenin Llwyd. The Grey King."

Grey Fox

Nobody else could feel it, Will knew. As far as outward appearances went, there was no reason why anybody should feel the least unease. The skies were a gentle light blue; the sun shone with unseasonable warmth, so that Rhys sat up on the tractor bare-backed as he ploughed the last stubbly fields, singing a clear tenor over the roar of the machine. The earth smelled clean. Yarrow and ragwort starred the hedgerows white and yellow, with the red berries of the hawthorn thick above them; the sweeping slopes where the valley began to rise were golden-brown with bracken, dry as tinder in this strange Indian-summer sun. Hazy on the horizon all around, the mountains lay like sleeping animals, their muted colours changing with every hour of the day from brown to green to purple and softly back again.

Yet behind all this autumnal gentleness, as he roamed the fields and the gorse-starred mountain, Will could feel tension mounting everywhere, advancing like a slow relentless flood from the high peaks brooding over the end of the valley. Enmity was beginning to push at him. Slowly but irresistibly, the pressure of malevolence was building up to the point where it could break and overwhelm him. And nobody else knew. Only the hidden senses of an Old One could feel the working of the Dark.

Aunt Jen was delighted with the change in Will's appearance. "Look at you — only a few days, but you have colour in your cheeks now, and if this sun goes on you will be getting brown. I was writing to Alice last night. I said, you wouldn't know him, he looks like a different boy —"

"Very nice sun, indeed," Will's Uncle David said. "But a little too much, for this time of year, thank you. The pastures are getting dry, and the bracken on the mountain — we could do with a bit of rain, now."

"Hark at you," Aunt Jen said, laughing. "Rain is one thing we are never short of here."

But still the sunny skies smiled, and Will went off with John Rowlands and his dogs to fetch a flock of yearling sheep that was to be wintered at Clwyd Farm. The hill farmer who owned them had already driven them down halfway to another farm at the head of the valley. As he looked at the milling off-white chaos of woolly backs, bobbing and shoving, eighty or so lusty young ewes bleating and baahing in ear-splitting chorus, Will could not imagine how they could possibly be brought intact to Clwyd. When just one sheep broke away from the rest and pranced sideways towards him, where he stood in the field, he could not persuade it back to its fellows even by yelling and pushing and whacking its broad woolly sides. "Baaaa," said the sheep, in a deep stupid baritone, as if he had not been there, and it wandered off and began chewing at the hedge. Yet the instant that Tip, John Rowlands's sheepdog, trotted purposefully in its direction, the sheep turned dutifully round and bobbed back to the rest.

Will could not see how John Rowlands communicated with his dogs. There were two: the dappled Tip, named for the splashes of white on his muzzle and the very end of his waving tail, and a bigger, more formidable-looking dog called Pen, with a black, long-haired coat and a crooked ear, torn in some fight long ago. Rowlands needed to do no more than look at them, a smile creasing his lean brown face, with a soft word in Welsh, or a quick whistle, and they would be off on some complicated manoeuvre that the average man could have understood only after ten minutes of detailed explanation.

"Walk at the front," he called to Will through the deep, unnerving chorus of baaas, as he opened the gate and the sheep poured through into the road like milk. "Well forward, to wave at any cars coming and stop them at the side."

Will blinked in alarm. "But how do I keep the sheep back? They'll all run past me!"

John Rowlands's grin flashed white in the dark Welsh face. "Don't worry. Pen will see to them."

And so Pen did; it was as if he had a rope tied round the front of the herd of sheep to keep it in a neat tight curve. Trotting, darting, slinking on his belly, moving always forward, sometimes persuading an errant sheep in the right direction with a curt single bark, he kept them all moving obediently along the road. And Will, clutching the stick John Rowlands had given him, strode ahead bursting with confident pride, feeling as if he had been a real shepherd since time began.

They met only two cars, in fact, all the way down the valley road, but directing even those two to pull in beside the hedge was enough pleasure, with the sheep crowding by in a rippling grey flood. Will was enjoying his job so much that perhaps, he thought afterwards, he let his deeper watchfulness falter. For when the attack came, he had no sense of warning at all.

They were on a lonely part of the road, with barren moorland on one side of the road and dark tree-clad mountainside rising at the other. No fields were cultivated here. Bracken and rocks fringed the roadside as if it were a track over the open mountain. Suddenly Will became aware of a change in the sound of the sheep behind him: a higher note of alarm in their bleating, a flurry of scuffing hooves. He thought at first that it must be John Rowlands and Tip, heading off a runaway; but then he heard a sharp, piercing whistle that in a moment had Pen swinging round at the sheep, growling, barking, threatening them to a standstill. And he heard John Rowlands calling: "Will! Quick! Will!"

He ran back, skirting the frightened bleating sheep; then jerked to a halt. Halfway past the flock, at the edge of the road, there was a great splash of red at the throat of a single tottering animal, smaller than the rest. Will saw a flicker of movement in the bracken as some unseen creature fled. Away it went towards the mountain, and the fronds waved and then were still. Will watched horrified as the wounded sheep staggered sideways and fell. Its fellows pushed away from it, terrified; the dogs growled and threatened, frantically containing the herd, and Will heard John Rowlands yelling, and the thwacking of his stick against the hard road. He too yelled and waved his arms at the heaving flock of sheep, keeping them together as they tried in panic to break away over the moor, and gradually the nervous animals calmed and were still.

John Rowlands was bending over the injured ewe.

Will shouted, across the heaving backs, "Is it all right?"

"Not much hurt. Missed the vein. We're lucky." Rowlands bent down, heaved the inert sheep over his shoulders and grasped its fore and hind feet separately, so that it hung across the back of his neck like a huge muffler. Grunting with effort, he slowly stood up; his neck and cheek were smeared red by the sheep's blood-stained fleece.

Will came towards him. "Was it a dog?"

Rowlands could not move his head, because of the sheep, but his bright eyes swivelled quickly round. "Did you see a dog?"

"No."

"Are you sure?"

"I saw something running away through the bracken, but I couldn't tell what it was. I just thought it must be a dog — I mean, what else could it have been?"

Rowlands did not answer, but waved him ahead and whistled to the dogs. The flock began pouring on down the road. He walked at the side of it now, leaving the rear entirely to Tip; neatly and efficiently the dog kept the sheep moving along.

Soon they came to a deserted cottage set back from the road: stone-walled, slate-roofed, sturdy-looking, but with the glass broken in its two small windows. John Rowlands kicked open the heavy wooden door, staggered inside, and came out without the sheep, breathing heavily and wiping his face on his sleeve. He closed the door. "Be safe there until we can get back to her," he called to Will. "Not far now."

Before long they were at Clwyd. Will opened the gate of the broad pasture where he knew the sheep were to be kept, and the dogs nudged and nagged them inside. For a few moments the sheep eddied about, bleating and muttering; then they settled down to a greedy rasping nibble of the lush grass.

John Rowlands fetched the Land-Rover and took Will with him to collect the injured sheep; at the last moment the black dog Pen leaped up into the car and settled down between Will's feet. Will rubbed his silky ears.

"It must have been a dog attacked that sheep, surely?" he said as they drove.

Rowlands sighed. "I hope not. But indeed, I cannot think of any wild creature that would attack a flock, with men and dogs alongside. Nothing but a wolf would do that, and there have been no wolves in Wales for two hundred years or more."

They drew up outside the cottage. Rowlands turned the car so that its back door would be in easy reach, and went into the little stone building.

He was out again almost at once, empty-handed, looking uneasily about him. "She's gone!"

"Gone!"

"There must be some sign — Pen! *Tyrd yma!*" John Rowlands went casting around outside the cottage, peering intently at grass and bracken and gorse, and the black dog wove its way round and about him, nose down. Will too peered hopefully, looking for flattened plants or signs of wool, or blood. He saw nothing. A jagged rock of white quartz glittered before them in the sunshine. A woodlark sang. Then all at once, Pen gave one short sharp bark and was off on a scent, trotting confidently, head down, through the grass.

They followed. But Will was puzzled, and he could see the same bafflement on John Rowlands's seamed face — for the dog was tracking through untouched grass, not a stem bent by the passing even of a small creature, let alone a sheep. There was the sound of water running somewhere ahead of them, and soon they came to a small stream flowing down towards the river, the jutting rocks in its course showing how much lower than usual it was running in the dry spell.

Pen paused, cast up and down the stream unsuccessfully, and came to John Rowlands whining.

"He's lost it," the shepherd said. "Whatever it was. Could have been no more than a rabbit, of course — though not too many rabbits I have ever heard tell of would have the sense to hide their trail in running water."

Will said: "But what happened to the sheep? It was hurt, it couldn't have walked away."

"Particularly through a closed door," Rowlands said drily.

"That's right, of course! D'you think whatever animal attacked it would have been clever enough to come back and drag it away?"

"Clever enough, perhaps," Rowlands said, staring back at the cottage. "But not strong enough. A yearling will weigh about a hundred pounds, I near broke my back carrying her a little way. You'd need a mighty big dog to drag that weight."

Will heard himself say, "Two dogs?"

John Rowlands looked at him with narrowed eyes. "You have some unexpected ideas, Will, for one not brought up on a farm . . . yes, two dogs together could drag a sheep. But how would they do it without leaving a great flat trail? And anyway, how could two or twenty dogs open that door?"

"Goodness knows," Will said. "Well — perhaps it wasn't any animal. Perhaps somebody drove by and heard the sheep bleating and got it out of the cottage and took it away. I mean they couldn't know we were coming back."

"Aye," John Rowlands said. He did not sound convinced. "Well, if any did that, we shall find the sheep at home when we get there, for it has the Pentref mark on its ear and any local man would know that we winter William Pentref's ewes. Come on, now." He whistled to Pen.

They were silent on the drive home, each lost deep in concern and baffled conjecture. John Rowlands, Will knew, was worrying over the need to find the sheep quickly, to doctor its wounds. He, Will, had his own worries. Although he had not mentioned it to Rowlands, and hardly dared even to think what it might mean, he knew that in the moment when the wounded sheep had staggered and fallen beside the flock, he had seen something more than that formless twitch of motion in the bracken where the attacker fled. He had seen the flash of a silvery body, and the muzzle of what had looked very much like a white dog.

Music was flowing out of the farmhouse in a golden stream, as if the sun were inside the window, shining out. Will paused, astonished, and stood listening. Somebody was playing a harp, long rippling arpeggios soaring out like birdsong; then without a break the music changed to something like a Bach sonata, notes and patterns as precise as snowflakes. John Rowlands looked down at him with a smile for a moment, then pushed open the door and went in.

A side door was open into a little parlour that Will had never noticed before; it looked like a creaky-neat Best Room, tucked away from the big kitchen-living room where all the real life of the house went on. The music was coming from this parlour; Rowlands stuck his head round the door, and so did Will. Sitting there, running his hands over the strings of a harp twice his own height, was Bran.

He stopped, stilling the strings with his palms. "Hullo, then."

"Much better," said John Rowlands. "Very much better, that, today."

"Good," Bran said.

Will said, "I didn't know you could play the harp."

"Ah," Bran said solemnly. "Lot of things the English don't know. Mr Rowlands teaches me. He taught your auntie too, this is hers I'm at." He ran one finger across the lilting strings. "Freezing in the winter in this room, always, but it keeps better in tune than in the warm . . . Ah, Will Stanton, you don't know what a distinguished place you are in. This is the only farm in Wales where there are two harps. Mr Rowlands has one in his house too, you see." He nodded through the window, at the trio of farm cottages across the yard. "I practise there mostly. But Mrs Rowlands is busy cleaning today."

"Where is David Evans?" asked John Rowlands.

"In the yard with Rhys. Cowshed, I think."

"*Diolch*." He went out, preoccupied.

"I thought you'd be at school," Will said.

"Half-holiday. I forget why." Bran wore the protective smoky glasses even indoors; they made him look eccentric and unreal, the inscrutable dark circles taking all expression out of his pale face. He was wearing dark trousers too, and a dark sweater, making his white hair still more striking and unnatural. Will thought suddenly: *he must do it on purpose, he likes being different.*

"An awful thing happened," he said, and told Bran about the sheep. But again he left out the quick glimpse of the attacker that had made him think it was a white dog.

"Are you sure the sheep was alive when John left it?" Bran said.

"Oh, yes, I think so. There's always the chance someone just stopped and took it away. I expect John's checking."

"What a weird business," Bran said. He stood up, stretching. "I've had enough practising. Want to come out?"

"I'll go and tell Aunt Jen."

On the way out, Bran picked up his flat leather schoolbag from a chair beside the door. "I must drop this off at home. And put the kettle on for Da. He comes in for a cuppa, round about now, if he's working near by."

Will said curiously, "Does your mother work too?"

"Oh, she's dead. Died when I was a baby, I don't remember her at all." Bran gave him a strange sideways look. "Nobody told you about me, then?

My dad and I, we're a bachelor household. Mrs Evans is very nice, always. We eat supper at the farm, weekends. Of course, you haven't been here at a weekend yet."

"I feel as if I'd been here for weeks," Will said, putting his face up to the sun. Something in the way Bran spoke was making him oddly uneasy, and he did not want to think about it too closely. He pushed it to the back of his mind, to join that image of the flicker of a white muzzle through the bracken.

"Where's Cafall?" he said.

"Oh, he will be out with Da. Thinking I am still at school." Bran laughed. "The time we had when Cafall was young, trying to persuade him that school is for boys but not puppies. When I went to primary school in the village, he used to sit at the gate all day, just waiting."

"Where do you go now?"

"Tywyn Grammar. In a bus."

They scuffed their feet through the dust of the path down to the cottages, a path made by wheels, two ruts with hummocky grass growing between. There were three cottages but only two were occupied; now that he was closer, Will could see that the third had been converted into a garage. He looked beyond, up the valley, where the mountains rose blue-hazed and beautiful into the clear sky, and he shivered. Though the mystery of the wounded sheep had taken up the front of his mind for a while, the deeper uneasiness was swelling back again now. All around, throughout the countryside, he could feel the malevolence of the Dark growing, pushing at him. It could not focus upon him, follow him like the gaze of a great fierce eye; an Old One had the power to conceal himself so that his presence could not at once be sensed so precisely. But clearly the Grey King knew that he was bound to come, soon, from somewhere. They had their prophecies, as did the Light. The barriers had gone up, and were growing stronger every day. Will felt suddenly how strange it was for him to be the invader; for the Light to be advancing against the Dark. Always before, through all the centuries, it had been the other way round, with the powers of the Dark sweeping in fearsome recurrent attack over the land of men protected in gentleness by the Light. Always the Light had been the defenders of men, champions of all that the Dark came to overturn. Now, an Old One must deliberately reverse the long habit of mind; now he must find the thrust of attack, instead of the resolute sturdy defence which for so long had kept the Dark at bay.

But of course, he thought, this attack itself is a small part of a defence, to build resistance for that other last and most dreadful time when the Dark will come rising again. It is a quest, to awaken the last allies of the Light. And there is very little time.

Bran said suddenly, uncannily echoing the last thread of his thought, "Hallowe'en, tonight."

"Yes," Will said.

Before he could say more, they were at the door of the cottage; it was half-open, a low heavy door

61

set in the stone wall. At Bran's footsteps the dog Cafall came bounding out, a small white whirlwind, leaping and whining with pleasure, licking his hand. It was noticeable that he did not bark. From inside, a man's voice called, "Bran?" and began speaking in Welsh. Then as Will followed Bran through the door, the man speaking, standing shirt-sleeved at a table, turned in mid-sentence and caught sight of him. He broke off at once and said formally, "I beg your pardon."

"This is Will," Bran said, tossing his bag of books on the table. "Mr Evans's nephew."

"Yes. I thought perhaps it was. How do you do, young man?" Bran's father came forward, holding out his hand; his gaze was direct and his handshake firm, though Will had an immediate curious feeling that the real man was not there behind the eyes. "I am Owen Davies. I have been hearing about you."

"How d'you do, Mr Davies," said Will. He was trying not to look surprised. Whatever he had expected in Bran's father, it was not this man: a man so completely ordinary and unremarkable, whom you could pass in the street without noticing he had been there. Someone as odd as Bran should have had an odd father. But Owen Davies was all medium and average: average height, medium-brown hair in a medium quantity; a pleasant, ordinary face, with a slightly pointed nose and thin lips; an average voice, neither deep nor high, with the same precise enunciation that Will was beginning to learn belonged to all North Welshmen. His clothes were ordinary, the same shirt and trousers and boots that would be worn by anyone else on a farm. Even the dog that stood at his side, quietly watching them all, was a standard Welsh sheepdog, black-backed, white-chested, black-tailed, unremarkable. Not like Cafall: just as Bran's father was not at all like Bran.

"There is tea in the pot, Bran, if you would both like a cup," Mr Davies said. "I have had mine, I am off over to the big pasture. And I shall be going out tonight, there is a chapel meeting. Mrs Evans will give you your supper."

"That's good," Will said cheerfully. "He can help me with my homework."

"Homework?" said Bran.

"Oh, yes. This isn't just a holiday for me, you know. They gave me all kinds of work from school, so I shouldn't get behind. Algebra, today. And history."

"That will be very good," Mr Davies said earnestly, pulling on his waistcoat, "so long as Bran takes care to do his own work as well. Of course, I know he will do that. Well, it is nice to meet you, Will. See you later, Bran. Cafall can stay."

And he went out, nodding to them amiably but with complete seriousness, leaving Will to reflect that after all there was one thing about Owen Davies that was not altogether common; he had not a glimmer of laughter in him.

There was no expression in Bran's face. He said flatly, "My father is a big one for chapel. He is a deacon, and there are two or three meetings for him in the week. And we go twice on Sundays."

"Oh," Will said.

"Yes. Oh is right. Want a cup of tea?"

"Not really, thank you."

"Let's go out, then." With absentminded conscientiousness Bran rinsed out the teapot and left it neatly inverted on the draining-board. "*Tyrd yma*, Cafall."

The white dog bounded happily beside them as they crossed the fields, away from cottage and farm, up the valley towards the mountains and the lone near peak. It stood at a right angle to the mountain behind it, jutting into the flat valley floor.

"Funny how that rock sticks out like that," Will said.

"Craig yr Aderyn? That's special, it's the only place in Britain where cormorants nest inland. Not very far inland, of course. Four miles from the sea, we are here. Haven't you been over there? Come on, we've got time." Bran changed direction slightly. "You can see the birds fine from the road."

"I thought the road was that way," Will said, pointing.

"It is. We can cut across to it this way." Bran opened a gate on to a footpath, crossed the path and scrambled over the wall on the other side. "The only thing is, you must go quietly," he said with a grin. "This is Caradog Prichard's land."

"Hush, Cafall," Will said in a heavy stage-whisper, turning his head. But the dog was not there. Will paused, puzzled. "Bran? Where's Cafall?"

Bran whistled. They both stood waiting, looking back at the long sweep of the slate-edged stone wall along the stubbled field. Nothing moved. The sun shone. Far away, sheep called. Bran whistled again, with no result. Then he went back, with Will close behind, and they climbed over the wall again and went down to the footpath they had crossed.

Bran whistled a third time, and called in Welsh. There was concern in his voice.

Will said, "Wherever could he have gone? He was right behind me when I came over the wall."

"He never does this. Never. He will never go from me without permission, or not come when he is called." Bran gazed anxiously up and down the footpath. "I don't like it. I shouldn't have let him come so near Mr Prichard's land. You and me is one thing, but Cafall —" He whistled again, loud and desperate.

"You don't suppose —" Will said. He stopped.

"That Prichard would shoot him, the way he said?"

"No, I was going to say, you don't suppose Cafall wouldn't come because he knew he shouldn't go on Mr Prichard's land. But that's silly, no dog could work out something like that."

"Oh," Bran said unhappily, "dogs can work out things a lot more complicated than that. I don't know. Let's try this way. It leads to the river."

They set off along the path, away from the looming mass of the rock Craig yr Aderyn. Somewhere ahead of them, a long way off, a dog barked.

"Is that him?' Will said hopefully.

Bran's white head was cocked on one side. The dog barked again, closer. "No. That's John Rowlands's big dog, Pen. But Cafall might have gone that way when he heard him —'

They both broke into a run, along the stony, grass-patched path. Will very soon lost his breath and dropped behind. Bran disappeared round a bend in the path ahead of him. When Will turned the corner himself, two things slammed simultaneously into his consciousness: the sight of Bran — without Cafall — talking to his father and John Rowlands, and the sick certainty that something evil had taken control of everything that was happening now on Clwyd Farm. It was a recognition, like the sudden sensing of an overwhelming sound or smell.

He came panting up to them, as Bran said: ". . . heard Pen bark, and thought he might have come this way, so we came running."

"And you saw nothing at all?" Owen Davies said. His face was tight with some deep concern. Looking at it, Will felt foreboding clutch at the pit of his stomach.

John Rowlands said, his deep voice strained, "And you, Will? Did you see anyone, anything, on the path just now?'

Will stared. "No. Only Cafall, before, and now we've lost him."

"No creature came past you?"

"Nothing at all. Why? What's wrong?"

Owen Davies said, bleakly, "In the big pasture up the way, there are four dead sheep with their throats torn out, and there is no gate open or any sign of what can have attacked them."

Will looked in horror at John Rowlands. "Is it the same —"

"Who can tell?" said the shepherd bitterly. Like Davies, he seemed caught between distress and rage. "But it is not dogs, I do not see how it could be dogs. It looks more like the work of foxes, though how that can be, I do not know."

"The *milgwn*, from the hills," said Bran.

"Nonsense," his father said.

"The what?" said Will.

"The *milgwn*," Bran said. His eyes were still darting round in search of Cafall, and he spoke automatically. "Grey foxes. Some of the farmers say there are big grey foxes that live up in the mountains, bigger and faster than our red foxes down here."

Owen Davies said, "That is nonsense. There are no such things. I have told you before, I will not have you listening to those rubbishy old tales."

His tone was sharp. Bran shrugged.

But across the front of Will's mind there came suddenly a brilliant image, clear as a film thrown on a screen: he saw three great foxes trotting in line, enormous grey-white animals with thick coats growing to the broadness of a ruff round their necks, and full brush-like tails. They moved across a hillside, among rocks, and for an instant one of them turned its head and looked full at him, with bright unwinking eyes. For that instant he could see them as clearly as he could see Bran. Then the image was gone, they were vanished, and he was standing again in the sunshine, mute, dazed, knowing that in one of the brief communications that can come — very rarely, only very rarely — unguarded from one Old One to another, his masters had sent him a warning picture of the creatures of the Grey King, agents of the Dark.

He said abruptly, "They aren't tales. Bran is right."

Bran stared at him, shaken by the crisp certainty in his voice. But Owen Davies looked across in chilly reproof, the corners of his thin mouth turned down. "Don't be foolish, boy," he said coldly. "What can you know of our foxes?"

Will never knew what he could have said in answer, for breaking into the tense stillness of the sunlit afternoon came a shout from John Rowlands, urgent, loud.

"*Tân!* Look over there! There is fire on the mountain! Fire!"

Fire on the Mountain

There was not much smoke, for so much fire. In a line along the lower slope of the mountain, which they could only just see above the hedge from where they stood, flames were blazing in the bracken. It was like a long wound, a gash in the peaceful brown slope, quivering with deadly, ominous life. Yet there was little colour in it, and they were too far away to hear any sound. For a moment Will was conscious only of wonder that John Rowlands should have caught sight of it at all.

Then they were deep in instructions, and the urgency of Rowlands's soft voice. "Off to the farm, both of you, quick. Call the fire from Tywyn and the police, and then come back with anyone who is there. All the hands you can get. And bring more fire brooms, Bran, you know where they are. Come on, Owen."

Both men ran up the path across the valley, and the boys dived for the gate that led over the fields

69

to Clwyd Farm. Bran swung his head round in a whirl of white hair: "Take it *gently*, now," he said earnestly, "or you'll be worse ill —" and he was off like a sprinter, leaving Will to close the gate and trot resignedly in his wake.

The telephoning was done by the time he caught Bran up at the farm. David Evans took them with him in the Land-Rover, with Rhys and a tall thin farmer called Tom Ellis who had been there when they arrived. The back of the little car had been hastily filled with fire brooms and sacking, and several buckets that Will's uncle seemed to have small hope of using. The dogs, for once, were left behind.

"They will be no good with fire," Rhys said, seeing Will cock his head to the plaintive barking. "And the sheep can get out of the way on their own — indeed they will all be well away, by now."

"I wonder where Cafall is," Will said, and then caught sight of Bran's face and wished he had not.

Close to, the fire on the mountain was very much more alarming than it had seemed from a distance. They could smell it now, and hear it; smell the smoke more bitter than a farm bonfire; hear the soft, dreadful sound of flames consuming the bracken, like paper crumpled in the hand, and the sudden crackling roar as a bush or a patch of gorse went up. And they could see the flames, leaping high, bright red and yellow at the edges of the fire but ferocious and near-invisible at its heart.

As they tumbled out of the car David Evans was yelling for the fire brooms. Will and Bran pulled them out: besoms made like those for old-fashioned sweeping, but with the twigs longer and wider-spread. John Rowlands and Bran's father, already equipped, were thrashing at the leading edge of the fire, trying to contain it; but the wind was gusting higher, and the flames, now leaping, now creeping, were soon past them and travelling along the lower edge of the mountain. As they swept upwards, roaring up the hillside through the tinder-dry bracken, Owen Davies jumped out of the way only just in time.

The crackling rose; the air was full of fumes and smoke and whirling black specks of charcoal and ash. Great heat shone out at them. They were all in a line beating at the flames, flailing away with all their might, yet only occasionally extinguishing a spark. John Rowlands shouted something desperately in Welsh; then seeing Will's uncomprehending face near him, gasped out: "We must drive it higher, before it can reach Prichard's! Keep it from the rock!"

Peering ahead at the great outsweeping rocky slope of Craig yr Aderyn, Will glimpsed for the first time the corner of a grey stone building jutting out beyond its far side. The light glinted on a spray of water flung up beside the house; someone was soaking the land all round it, in an effort to deaden the fire if it should reach that far. But Will, beating hopelessly with his long flat-tipped broom, felt that nothing could halt or check the inferno before them, snarling high over their heads now as it reached a tangle of blackberry bushes. It was like a huge beast raging over the mountain, gobbling up everything in its path with irresistible greed. It was so powerful, and they so small, that even the effort to control its path seemed ludicrous. He thought: *It is like the Dark* — and for the first time found himself wondering how the fire could have begun.

Below them, from the road past the foot of the great Craig, came the clanging of a fire engine's bell, and Will glimpsed patches of bright red through the trees, and a hose snaking through the air. Men's voices were calling faintly and there was a sound of engines. But up here on the slope, the fire was gaining a greater hold, as the gusting wind caught it in patches, and gradually they were forced downwards, into the trees edging the road. In triumphant thunder the fire roared after them.

"Down the road!" the thin man Tom Ellis called. "Those trees will catch in a minute!"

Will panted along at John Rowlands's side. "What will happen?"

"Burn itself out, eventually." But the Welshman's creased face was grim.

Bran came trotting up at his other side, his white skin smudged and dirty. "This wind is the trouble, taking it up the valley — is Prichard's place really in danger, Mr Rowlands?"

John Rowlands checked his stride for a moment, to gaze all round the sky. Clouds were forming in the blue air now, strange ragged dirty-white clouds that seemed to be coming from no one direction. "I don't know . . . the wind is for a change in the weather, and it is shifting, but hard to tell where . . . we shall have rain sooner or later."

"Well," Will said hopefully, "the rain will put the fire out, won't it?" But as he spoke, he could hear the crackle and roar of the fire like laughter at his back, and he was not surprised when John Rowlands shook his head.

"Only a great deal of rain . . . the ground is so dry, dry as it never is this time of year — nothing but a downpour will have any effect at all." He looked round again, frowning at the mountains and the sky. "Something is strange, about this fire and everything . . . something is wrong . . ." He shook his shoulders, giving up the search, and strode on ahead as they rounded a bend and came towards the fire engine and its thunderous thrumming engine.

Will thought: *Ah, John Rowlands, you see more than you think you see, though not quite enough. The Dark Lord has begun his work in these mountains, the Grey King is building up a wall to enclose the golden harp, and the Sleepers who must be wakened, so that it may not come to them and fulfil the quest. For if he can keep them from the reach of the Light, then the Old Ones will not come into their full power, and there will be none to keep the Dark from rising . . .*

He said, without knowing that he spoke aloud: "But it won't work!"

A voice said softly in his ear, "What won't work?" Bran's dark smoky spectacles, shrouding the eyes behind, were staring into his face.

Will looked at him and said with sudden naked honesty, "I don't know what to make of you."

"I know you don't." Bran said, a quirk of a smile twitching his strange pale face. "But you're going to need me all the same." He spun round, as smoke from the fire up the hillside came billowing down around them. "Don't worry," he said, grinning. "Nobody else has ever known what to make of me either." And he was off, spinning, running, almost dancing up the road towards the fire engine.

Will ran after him. And then in a moment both of them were brought up short by a sight more astonishing than any yet. Beneath the looming bulk of Craig yr Aderyn the firemen had two hoses playing, drenching both the mountain and the side of the road in an effort to check the fire from leaping over the Craig and down to Prichard's Farm. Others ran here and there with buckets, fire brooms, anything with which stray sparks might be drowned or beaten out before they gained a hold. The road was buzzing with anxious activity. Yet in the midst of it all, standing rigid and oblivious with fury, stood Caradog Prichard, his red hair bristling, blood on his shirt and a shotgun levelled in one hand — and the other hand out rigid, pointing in accusation as he screamed with rage at John Rowlands.

"Bring me the dog! Bring him! I will prove to you that it was him, him and that freakish white hound of the freak boy Davies! I will show you! Six sheep in my field, there are six of them, with their throats ripped out, dammo, their heads half off — all for black joy, and that is what those bloody dogs had of it and that is what I shall shoot them for! Bring me them here! Bring them! And I will prove it to you!"

The boys stood frozen, gazing at him in horror; he was not for that moment a human being, but a frenzied creature possessed by rage, turned into an animal. All that could be seen in him was the urge to hurt, and it was, as it always will be, the most dreadful sight in the world.

Looking at Prichard with the eye of a human and the vision of an Old One, Will was filled with an overpowering compassion: an awareness of what must inevitably overtake Caradog Prichard if he were not checked, now, for always, in this passion before it was too late. Stop, he longed to call to him: stop, before the Grey King sees you and puts out his hand in friendship, and you, unwitting, take it and are destroyed ...

Before he thought what he was doing he stepped forward, and the movement brought the red-haired man swinging towards him. The finger wheeled viciously round, jabbing at him through the air.

"You there too, *Sais bach*, you are part of it, you and your uncle's farm. They are Clwyd dogs, these murdering brutes, it is on all your heads, and I will have my due from all of you, from all of you —"

75

Spittle foamed at the corners of his mouth. There was no speaking to him. Will fell back, and with the fury of Prichard's shouting even the firefighters paused in amazement. There was no sound but the thump of the fire engine's pumping and the crackle of the approaching flames, and no movement for an instant anywhere. Then David Evans pushed forward, a small brisk form with a fire broom in his hand and smudges of soot on his face and shirt, and he took Prichard fearlessly by the shoulder and shook him, hard.

"The fire will be on us in minutes, Caradog Prichard — do you want your farm to burn? All of us here working our hands raw to keep the flames from your roof, and your wife inside there doing the same, and you stand here shouting your silly head off and think of nothing but a few dead sheep! A lot more dead sheep you will have, man, and a dead farm too, if you do not pull yourself together now. Now!"

Prichard gazed blankly at him, the small bright eyes squinting suspiciously in the pudgy face, and then he seemed gradually to wake up, and to realize where he was and what was happening. Dazed, he stared at the flames leaping closer beyond the hedge. The pump of the fire engine rose to a higher pitch, as the workers swung their hoses round to meet the advancing fire; sparks flew in all directions as the beaters thwacked frantically at the bracken. Caradog Prichard gave one short squeal of terror, turned, and rushed back towards his farmhouse.

Without a word Will and Bran rejoined the line of beaters, edging diagonally up the hillside in an effort to keep the fire from sweeping over and beyond the Craig. The sky was growing darker as the clouds thickened and the evening drew on, but there was no hint of rain. Again the wind gusted, dropped to nothing, rose in a sudden new gust; there was no telling what it would do next. More and more strongly Will could feel the enmity of the Grey King thrusting at him from the high peaks at the head of the valley; it made a wall as fierce as the wall of flames roaring towards them from the other direction, though the only one who could feel the force of both, the only one caught between the two, was the Old One, Will Stanton, bound by birth to follow this quest wherever it might lead ... He was swept up suddenly in a wild exhilaration, bringing energy from nowhere to harden his drooping arms and legs. Yelling with sudden glee, grinning madly at Bran, he whacked at the flames licking the bracken at his feet as if he could flatten them in an instant into the ground.

Then a flash of movement higher up the mountain caught his eyes away from the line of flame, and out of the bare rocks above he saw, flinging itself forward at astonishing speed, the form of a grey-white fox. Brush flying out behind, ears back; it leapt up the towering side of Craig yr Aderyn. Smoke billowed, rising on the wind, and the fox was gone. Will had seen it for only a quick moment.

He heard a high wail from Bran. "Cafall!"

Then the Welsh boy was scrambling up the slope, ignoring cries of concern from below, ignoring the fire and the smoke and all else except the glimpse of the white animal he had thought was his dog.

"Bran, come back! It isn't Cafall!"

Will climbed desperately after him, his heart thumping as if it would leap out of his chest. "Bran! Come back!"

Steeper and steeper the slope grew, until they were upon the Craig itself, scrambling through bracken, over slippery grass, round jutting shelves of grey rock. Bran paused at last on one of these, panting, staring wildly about him. Will stumbled up beside him, hardly able to speak.

"Cafall!" Bran shouted into nowhere.

"It wasn't Cafall, Bran."

"Of course it was. I saw him."

"It was a fox, Bran. One of the *milgwn*. Bran, it's a trick, don't you see?"

Will coughed, choking in a billowy gust of smoke from the black cloud that wreathed round the slope behind and below them. They could see nothing but smoke and the steep rock, with patches of grey sky above their heads. Below, there was no sign of the farm or men or the valley, and in their ears no sound but the sighing of the wind, and somewhere the harsh faint voices of birds.

Bran looked at Will uncertainly.

"Bran, I'm sure of it."

"All right. I was so certain . . . I'm sorry."

"Don't be. It wasn't you seeing. It was the Grey King making you see. But the trouble is, we can't go back that way, the fire's coming up after us —"

"There is a way down the other side," Bran said, brushing sweat from his eyes. "No bracken for the fire to burn there, just rock. But it's hard going." He looked doubtfully at Will's pale smudged face.

"I'm all right. Go on, go on."

They clambered on up the rough stairway of grass and rock, holding on now with both hands and feet.

"There's a bird's nest here!" Will had glimpsed an untidy pile of twigs and bracken a foot from his head.

"There'd be birds too, if it weren't for the fire. It's a nesting place in spring, I told you. Not just the cormorants — ravens too. Lots of birds . . . which is why they call it Bird Rock, of course. Here —" Bran paused upright on a broad shelf of rock, edged with bracken. "This is the ridge. It goes down the other side towards Prichard's Farm."

But Will was standing very still, looking at him. "Bird Rock?"

"That's right," Bran said, surprised. "Bird Rock. Craig yr Aderyn, rock of the birds. I thought you knew that."

Will said softly, reflectively:

"On the day of the dead, when the year too dies,
Must the youngest open the oldest hills
Through the door of the birds, where the breeze
     breaks . . ."

Bran stared at him. "You mean . . . the door of the birds . . . here?"

"Bird Rock. It must be. I know it. And this is the day of the dead —" Will swung his head sharply, gazing up at the sky where clouds flew like grey puffs of smoke. "And the wind's changing, feel . . . No . . . Yes, there again . . . A bad wind, a wind from the Dark. I don't like it, Bran, it has the Grey King in it." He spoke now with no thought of Bran as anything but an ally, ever.

The white-haired boy said bleakly, "It's swinging to the north. That is the worst wind of all, the north wind. *Gwynt Traed yr Meirw*, they call it, the wind that blows round the feet of the dead. It brings storms. And worse, sometimes."

The distant crackling of the fire seemed louder now. Will glanced over his shoulder, down the hill; the smoke was thicker there, and he felt more heat in the air. The wind whirled in gusts, catching up cinders and soot from below into strange dark eddies round their heads. All at once Will knew with dreadful certainty that the Grey King was aware of him, precisely aware, gathering his power for attack — and that it was at that first moment of awareness that the fire on the mountain had begun. He flinched in a sudden sense of fearful loneliness. An Old One, alone without others of the Light, was vulnerable to the Dark at its strongest. Though he could not be destroyed for all time, yet he could be disarmed; the full power of a Lord of the Dark could, if it struck him defenceless, blast him out of

Time for so great a space that he could be of no help to his fellows until too late. So the Grey King struck now at Will with fire and with all else that might be at his command.

And Bran was more vulnerable yet. Will swung back quickly. "Bran, come on, along the ridge to the top. Before the fire —"

His voice died in his throat. Silently on to the ridge round them, out of holes and crevices, round corners and crags, came slinking the grey-white ghostly shapes of the *milgwn*, more than a score of them: heads held low, teeth grinning, a white tip glimmering on each stiffly-held grey bushy tail. Their foxy smell was in the air stronger than the smoke. At their head stood the king fox, their leader, red tongue lolling from a mouth set in a wide dreadful grin, its white teeth long as fingers and sharp as nails, icicles of bone. The eyes were bright; the ruff stood out white round the huge shoulders and neck.

Will clenched his fists, shouting angry words of power in the Old Speech, but the great grey fox did not flinch. Instead it made a sudden sharp leap into the air, straight up on the one spot, as Will had once seen a fox do in a Buckinghamshire field, far away from this valley, to discover what danger lurked in a field of wheat higher than its head. As it jumped, the king fox gave one short, sharp bark, deep and clear. The *milgwn* snarled low. And an abrupt *whoof* of flame shot up at Will's side with a sound like tearing cloth, as the fire on the mountain burst at last on the ridge of Craig yr Aderyn and roared crackling round them in the bracken.

Will shrank back. There was no way of escape but past the king fox. And the big fox crouched motionless, low on its belly, tensing itself to spring.

There was a sudden piercing yell at Will's shoulder. Bran leapt forward, waving in his hand a crooked branch of scrub oak blazing like tinder, a sheaf of flame; he thrust it full into the grey fox's face. Screaming, the animal fell back amongst its fellows, and the foxes milled in confusion. Before the branch could burn down to his arm, Bran flung it aside. But unexpectedly, caught by a gust of wind, it fell over the opposite side of the ridge, down towards the unburned slope. Out it went and over the edge, and down to the far side of the Craig where the fire might not otherwise have gone. There was a gasp of flame as the fire took hold on its new prey. Bran wailed in horror.

"Will! I've been and sent the fire down to Prichard's Farm — we're cut off both ways!"

"The top!" Will called urgently. "We must get to the top!" With all the certainty of ancient instincts he knew the place they must find; it had begun compellingly to call to him, unseen, waking to his quest. He knew what it would look like; he knew what he must do when they reached it. But the reaching was another matter. Flames crackled at either side of them, scorching their dry skin; ahead, the *milgwn* gathered now in a tight semicircle, waiting, waiting —

Desperately Will put protection about himself and Bran, standing foursquare facing the north and calling some words in the Old Speech: it was the Spell of Helledd, to give freedom to a wanderer against any compulsion by those holding the land over which he roamed. But there was not much hope in him; he knew it could not hold for long. Beside him he heard Bran give a great imploring shout, like a small child calling for help without knowing that he calls.

"Cafall! Cafall!"

And out of nowhere along the ridge towards them came a white streak, leaping at the nearest fox, charging it sideways, so that it spun round with a shriek rolling over and over. The tight semicircle wavered, uncertain. Cafall leapt snarling at the next fox, his jaws closing quick and hard on its shoulder, and the animals squealed dreadfully and twisted away. There in the rent he had torn in the rank of the *milgwn* the white dog stood, belligerent as a bull, with his legs planted firm on the rock, and the message glinting in his strange silvery eyes was clear. Will grabbed Bran by the arm and slipped out with him past Cafall, free, while the panting foxes hesitated.

"Up here, Bran, quick! It's the only place!"

Bran's eyes flickered over black earth and white fur, dark hills and grey sky; he saw the great king fox of the *milgwn* watching them, controlled again, poised for pursuit. Then Cafall, curving to face the animal, began a long crescendo snarl more bloodcurdling than any sound Bran had ever heard in his life. In fulfilment of some long destiny, the dog was making it possible for them to escape. There was no excuse not to obey. With a sudden flooding of trust and humility, Bran turned and scrambled upwards after Will.

Clambering on hands and feet over the rocky ridge, Will made for the place to which they must go; it sang to him, beckoning. Below the rocks to which they clung, smoke swirled like a dark sea; high above, unseen birds screamed and cawed in angry fear. When he could climb no further, Will saw a narrow overhung cleft in the rocks before him, a long slit broadened and eroded by frost and wind and rain. Its grey granite sides were green-patched with lichen. Irresistibly, it summoned him.

He called to Bran: "In here!" Then his voice rose louder, commanding. "Cafall!"

The granite sides of the cleft towered three times higher than his head. Entering, Will glanced back over his shoulder; he saw Bran following, bemused, and then a quick white shape slipping after him, as Cafall darted forward, nuzzling his nose briefly into Bran's hand as he passed. Outside on the rock, a shrieking tumult of baffled rage rose from the furious *milgwn*, prevented from entry. Their master's power, Will now knew, was a power over the rock and the mountains and all the high places of Gwynedd; but only over those. Inside the rock and the mountain was a different domain.

He went on. At its far end, the rocky cleft widened a little. The light was dim. Things seemed indistinct, as if in a dream. Outside, the foxes barked and screamed. And then there was nothing more ahead of Will but bare grey rock: a formidable blank wall, ending the cleft. Will stared at the rock, and his mind filled with a warmth of discovery and relief as intense as joy. The dog Cafall was at his side, standing straight and proud as a young horse. Will dropped one hand to rest on the white head. The other arm he raised before him, with fingers stiff outstretched in a gesture of command, and he called out three words in the Old Speech.

And before him, the rock parted like a great gate, to a faint, very faint sound of delicate music that was achingly familiar and yet strange, gone as soon as it was heard. Will walked forward through the rocky doors, with Cafall trotting confidently beside him, head high and tail waving. And Bran, a little hesitantly, followed them.

Bird Rock

There was no way of telling whether they were deep inside Craig yr Aderyn, or had walked through the grey rocky doors into another place and time. It did not matter to Will. Exhilaration was pulsing through him, in this the true beginning of his first full quest as an Old One. Turning to look back, he saw without surprise that the doors through which they had come were no longer there. The rocky wall at the end of the chamber where they now stood was smooth and unbroken, and upon it, high up, there hung a round golden shield, glinting dully in a light that came from somewhere deep within the room.

Will looked tentatively at Bran, but the Welsh boy seemed unperturbed. His pale face was oddly vulnerable without its protective glasses, but Will could read no expression in the catlike eyes; he felt once more an intense curiosity about this strange boy with no colour in him, born into the Dark-haunted valley — mortal, and yet also a creature foreknown by the Old Ones centuries before. How was it that he, Will, an Old One himself could sense so little of Bran's nature?

"You okay?" he said.

"I'm all right," said Bran. He was looking up at the walls, beyond Will. "*Duw*," he said softly. "Beautiful. Look at those."

It was a long, empty room. On its walls hung four tapestries, two to each side, their rich colours so deeply gleaming that they too seemed to shimmer in the half-light, like the golden shield. Will blinked in recognition at the images embroidered there, rich as stained glass: a silver unicorn, a field of red roses, a glowing golden sun . . .

All the light in this room seemed, he now saw, to come from only one flame. In an iron holder jutting from the stone wall near the end of the room, a single tremendous candle stood. It was several feet high, and it burned with a white unwavering flame of intense brilliance. The long shadow of the candle lay over wall and floor, motionless, undancing. Its stillness, Will realized, was the stillness of the High Magic, a power beyond Light or Dark or any allegiance — the strongest and most remote force in the universe, which soon in this place he and Bran must face.

There was a faint whistling whine at his side, scarcely audible. He looked down, and saw the dog Cafall gazing backwards at Bran.

Will said softly, "Go on, then."

The dog's cold nose nudged his hand, and Cafall turned and trotted briskly back to his master, waving his tail. Bran thrust his fingers into the fur of the dog's head in quick fierce affection, and Will knew that for all his calm appearance there was in his mind an uncertainty approaching panic, which Cafall had sensed and sought to reassure. Will felt a quick tug of sympathy for Bran, but there was no time for explanations. He knew he must trust his instinctive feeling that, in the last resort, the strange remoteness always apparent in Bran would prove to be the strangeness of great strength.

He said aloud, without turning, "This way." Then he walked firmly down the long lofty chamber. Bran followed with Cafall; Will could hear the footsteps ringing with his own on the stone-paved floor. He reached the tall candle in the wall. Its iron holder was set into the stone at the level of his shoulder; the smooth white sides of the candle reached far higher, high above his head, so that the white flame glowed up there like a bright full moon.

Will paused. "First the moon," he said. "Then stars and, if all is well, a comet, and then the dust of the stars. And at the last, the sun."

"What?" said Bran.

Will glanced across without really seeing. Behind his eyes he was looking into his own mind and memory, not at Bran. Here in this place he was an Old One, occupied with the affairs of the Light; nothing else had very much relevance. He said, "It is the order of things, by which the High Magic shall be known. So that none may come within reach of it except by birthright."

Bran said, "I still don't know what you're talking about." Then he shook his head in quick nervous apology. "I'm sorry, I didn't mean to sound —"

"It doesn't matter," Will said. "Just follow. You'll see."

The footsteps rang out again, and then they were at the end of the long room and there was nothing before them but a blank hole in the floor. Bran peered at it dubiously.

Will said, "Do what I do." He sat on the edge of the rough rectangular opening in the floor, and in a few moments he could see a staircase, running downwards at a steep angle. Cautiously lowering himself, he found the stairway was narrow and dark; it was like going down into a well. When he put out a hand to either side, each hand at once touched rock, and the rock of the roof too was very close to his head. He went slowly down. In a moment he could hear Bran's careful steps following, and the soft scratch of Cafall's paws. For a little while the glimmer from the upper chamber reached down after them, casting wavering patterns of shadow on the close walls, but soon even that faded, and there was no light in the stair tunnel at all. In its sides, Will's fingers found two smooth channels carved to form balustrades, a steadying refuge for the hands of anyone descending. He said quietly, his voice eerily echoing, "Bran, if you put your hands out —"

"I've found them," Bran said. "Like banisters, aren't they? Bright idea of somebody's, that." The words were cool, but there was tension behind them.

Their voices boomed gently in the stairway, muffled as if by mist.

Will said, "Go carefully. I may stop in a hurry." He was straining to hear the voice of his instincts; random images and impressions flickered in and out of his mind. Something was calling him, something close, close —

He put out a hand in front of him, just in time to save himself from coming hard up against a blank wall of rock. There was no other stair ahead: only a stony dead end.

"What is it?" said Bran, behind.

"Wait a moment." An instruction was growing inside Will's memory, like an echo from another world. Standing with his feet planted firmly on the last stair, he put the palms of both hands flat against the rough unseen rockface barring their way, and he pushed. At the same time he said certain words in the Old Speech that came into his mind.

And the rock parted, silently, as it had when the great doors opened silently on Bird Rock, though no music sounded here. With Bran and Cafall at his heels, Will stepped forward into a faint glow of light that caught him into such wonder that he could only stand and gaze.

They were no longer where they had been. They stood somewhere in another time, on the roof of the world. All around them was the open night sky, like a huge black inverted bowl, and in it blazed the stars, thousand upon thousand brilliant prickles of fire. Will heard Bran draw in a quick breath. They stood, looking up. The stars blazed round them. There was no sound anywhere, in all the immensity of space. Will felt a wave of giddiness; it was as though they stood on the last edge of the universe, and if they fell, they would fall out of Time . . . As he gazed about him, gradually he recognized the strange inversion of reality in which they were held. He and Bran were not standing in a timeless dark night observing the stars in the heavens. It was the other way around. They themselves were observed. Every blazing point in that great depthless hemisphere of stars and suns was focused upon them, contemplating, considering, judging. For by following the quest for the golden harp, he and Bran were challenging the boundless might of the High Magic of the universe. They must stand unprotected before it, on their way, and they would be allowed to pass only if they had the right by birth. Under that merciless starlight of infinity, any unrightful challenger would be brushed into nothingness as effortlessly as a man might brush an ant from his sleeve.

Will stood, waiting. There was nothing else that he could do. He looked for friends in the sky. He found the Eagle and the Bull, with Aldebaran glowing red and the Pleiades glimmering; he saw Orion brandish his club high, encouraging, with Betelgeuse and Rigel winking at shoulder and toe. He saw the Swan and the Eagle flying towards one another along the bright path of the Milky Way; he saw the hazy hint of distant Andromeda, and Earth's near neighbours Tau Ceti and Procyon, and Sirius the dog star. In longing hope Will gazed at them; in hope and in salutation, for during his time of learning the ways of an Old One he had flown amongst them all.

Then the sky wheeled, and the stars slanted and changed; now the Centaur galloped overhead, and the blue double star Acrux supporting the Southern Cross. The Hydra stretched lazily over the heavens, with the Lion marching by, and the great Ship sailed its leisurely, eternal way. And at last a brilliant point of light, with a long curving tail, came blazing into view over half the inverted bowl of the sky, moving past in a long stately progress; and Will knew that he and Bran had survived their first ordeal.

He pressed Bran's arm briefly, and saw a flicker of reflected light as the white head turned.

"It is a comet!" Bran whispered.

Will said softly back, "Wait. There's more, if all is well."

The long flaring tail of the comet moved gradually out of sight, down over the horizon of their nameless world and time. Still in the black hemisphere the stars blazed and slowly wheeled; beneath them, Will felt so infinitesimally small that it seemed impossible he should even exist. Immensity pressed in on him, terrifying, threatening — and then, in a swift flash of movement like dance, like the glint of a leaping fish, came a flick of brightness in the sky from a shooting star. Then another, and another, here, there, all around. He heard Bran give a small chirrup of delight, a spark struck from the same bright sudden joy that filled his own being. *Wish on a star*, said a tiny voice in his head from some long-departed day of early childhood: *Wish on a star —* the cry of a pleasure and faith as ancient as the eyes of man.

"Wish on a falling star," said Bran soft in his ear. All around them the meteors briefly dived and vanished, as tiny points of stardust in the long travel of their cloud struck the aery halo of the earth, burned bright and were gone.

I wish, said Will fiercely in his mind: *I wish ... Oh, I wish ...*

And all the bright starlit sky was gone, in a flicker of time that they could not catch, and darkness came around them so fast that they blinked in disbelief at its thick nothingness. They were back on the staircase beneath Bird Rock, with stone steps under their feet and a curved stone balustrade smooth to the sightless touch of their hands. And as Will stretched out one hand groping before him, he found no blank wall of stone there to bar his way, but free open space.

Slowly, faltering, he went on down the dark stairway, and Bran and Cafall followed him.

Then very gradually faint light began to filter up from below. Will saw a glimmer from the walls enclosing them; then the shape of the steps beneath his feet; then, appearing round a curve in the long tunnelling stairway, the bright circle that marked its end. The light grew brighter, the circle larger; Will felt his steps become quicker and more eager, and mocked himself, but could not help it.

Then instinct caught him into caution, and on the last few steps of the staircase, before the light, he stopped. Behind him he heard Bran and the dog stop too, at once. Will stood listening to his senses, trying to catch the source of warning. He saw, without properly seeing, that the steps on which they stood had been carved out of the rock with immense care and symmetry, perfectly angled, smooth as glass, every detail as clear as if the rock had been cut only the day before. Yet there was a noticeable hollow in the centre of each step, which could only have been worn by centuries of passing feet. Then he ceased to notice such things, for awareness caught at him out of the deepest corner of his mind and told him what he must do.

Carefully Will pushed up the left sleeve of his sweater as far as the elbow, leaving the forearm bare. On the underside of his arm shone the livid scar that had once been accidentally burned there like a brand: the sign of the Light, a circle quartered by a cross. In a deliberate slow gesture, half defensive, half defiant, he raised this arm crooked before his face, as if shielding his eyes from bright light, or warding off an unexpected blow. Then he walked down the last few steps of the staircase and out into the light. As he stepped to the floor, he felt a shock of sensation like nothing he had ever known. A flare of white brilliance blinded him, and was gone; a brief tremendous thunder dazed his ears, and was gone; a force like a blast wave from some great explosion briefly tore at his body, and was gone. Will stood still, breathing fast. He knew that beneath his singular protection, he had brought them through the last door of the High Magic: a living barrier that would consume any unsought intruder in a gasp of energy as unthinkable as the holocaust of the sun. Then he looked into the room before him, and for a moment of illusion thought that he saw the sun itself.

It was an immense cavernous room, high-roofed, lit by flaring torches thrust into brackets on the stone walls, and hazy with smoke. The smoke came from the torches. Yet in the centre of the floor burned a great glowing fire, alone, with no chimney or fireplace to contain it. It gave no smoke at all, but burned with a white light of such brilliance that Will could not look straight at it. No intense heat came from this fire, but the air was filled with the aromatic scent of burning wood, and there was the crackling, snapping sound of a log fire.

Will came forward past the fire, beckoning Bran to follow; then stopped abruptly as he saw what lay ahead.

Hazy at the end of the chamber three figures sat, in three great thrones that seemed to be fashioned out of smooth grey-blue Welsh slate. They did not move. They appeared to be men, dressed in long hooded robes of differing shades of blue. One robe was dark, one was light, and the robe between them was the shifting greenish-blue of a summer sea. Between the three thrones stood two intricately carved wooden chests. At first there seemed to be nothing else in the huge room, but after a moment of gazing Will knew that there was movement in the deep shadows beyond the fire, in the darkness all around the three illuminated lords. These were the bright figures on a dark canvas, lit to catch the eye; beyond them in the darkness other things of unknown nature lurked.

He could tell nothing of the nature of the three figures, beyond sensing great power. Nor could his senses as an Old One penetrate the surrounding darkness. It was as if an invisible barrier stood all around them, through which no enchantment might reach.

Will stood a little way before the thrones, looking up. The faces of the three lords were hidden in the shadows of their hooded robes. For a moment there was silence, broken only by the soft crackle of the burning fire; then out of the shadows a deep voice said, "We greet you, Will Stanton. And we name you by the sign. Will Stanton, Signseeker."

"Greetings," Will said, in as strong and clear a voice as he could muster, and he pulled down his sleeve over his scarred arm. "My lords," he said, "it is the day of the dead."

"Yes," said the figure in the lightest blue robe. His face seemed thin in the shadows of his hood, the eyes gleaming, and his voice was light, sibilant, hissing. "Yesssssss . . ." Echoes whispered like snakes out of the dark, as if a hundred other little hissing voices came from nameless shapes behind him, and Will felt the small hairs rise on the back of his neck. Behind him he heard Bran give a muffled involuntary moan, and knew that horror must be creeping like a white mist through his mind. Will's strength as an Old One rebelled. He said in quick cold reproach, "My lord?"

The horror fell away, like a cloud whisked off by the wind, and the lord in the light blue robe softly laughed. Will stood there frowning at him, unmoved: a small stocky boy in jeans and sweater, who nonetheless knew himself to possess power worthy of meeting these three. He said, confident now, "It is the day of the dead, and the youngest has opened the oldest hills, through the door of the birds. And has been let pass by the eye of the High Magic. I have come for the golden harp, my lords."

The second figure in the sea-blue robe said, "And the raven boy with you."

"Yes."

Will turned to Bran, standing hesitantly nearer the fire, and beckoned him. Bran came forward very slowly, feet as unwilling as if they swam against treacle, and stood at his side. The light from the torches on the walls shone in his white hair.

The lord in the sea-blue robe leaned forward a little from his throne; they glimpsed a keen, strong face and a pointed grey beard. He said, astonishingly, "Cafall?"

At Bran's side the white dog stood erect and quivering. He did not move an inch forward, as if obeying some inner instruction that told him his place, but his tail waved furiously from side to side as it never waved for anyone but Bran. He gave a soft, small whine.

White teeth glinted in the hooded face. "He is well named. Well named."

Bran said jealously, in sudden fierce anxiety, "He is my dog!" Then he added, rather muffled, "My lord." Will could feel the alarm in him at his own temerity.

But the laughter from the shadows was kindly. "Never fear, boy. The High Magic would never take your dog from you. Certainly the Old Ones would not either, and the Dark might try but would not succeed." He leaned forward suddenly, so that for an instant the strong, bearded face was clear; the voice softened, and there was an aching sadness in it. "Only the creatures of the earth take from one another, boy. All creatures, but men more than any. Life they take, and liberty, and all that another man may have — sometimes through greed, sometimes through stupidity, but never by any volition but their own. Beware your own race, Bran Davies — they are the only ones who will ever harm you, in the end."

Dread stirred in Will as he felt the deep sadness in the voice, for there was a compassion in it directed solely at Bran, as if the Welsh boy stood at the edge of some long sorrow. He had a quick sense of a mysterious closeness between these two, and knew that the lord in the sea-blue robe was trying to give Bran strength and help, without being able to explain why. Then the hooded figure leaned abruptly back, and the mood was gone.

Will said huskily, "Nevertheless, my lord, the rights of that race have always been the business of the Light. And in quest of them I claim the golden harp."

The soft-voiced lord in the lightest robe, who had spoken first, swiftly stood. His cloak swirled round him like a blue mist; bright eyes glinted from the pale face glimmering in the hood.

"Answer the three riddles as the law demands, Old One, you and the White Crow your helper there, and the harp shall be yours. But if you answer wrong, the doors of rock shall close, and you be left defenceless on the cold mountain, and the harp shall be lost to the Light forever."

"We shall answer," Will said.

"You, boy, the first." The blue mist swirled again. A bony finger was thrust pointing at Bran, and the shadowed hood turned. Will turned too, anxiously; he had half expected this.

Bran gasped. "Me? But — but I —"

Will reached out and touched his arm. He said gently, "Try. Only try. We are here only to try. If the answer is asleep in you, it will wake. If it is not, no matter. But try."

Bran stared at him unsmiling, and Will saw his throat move as he swallowed. Then the white head turned back again. "All right."

The soft, sibilant voice said, "Who are the Three Elders of the World?"

Will felt Bran's mind reel in panic, as he tried to find meaning in the words. There was no way to offer help. In this place, the law of the High Magic prevented an Old One from putting the smallest thought or image into another mind: Will was permitted only to overhear. So, tense, he stood overhearing the turmoil of his friend's thoughts, as they tossed about desperately seeking order.

Bran struggled. The Three Elders of the World . . . somewhere he knew . . . it was strange and yet familiar, as if somewhere he had seen, or read . . . the three oldest creatures, the three oldest things . . . he had read it at school, and he had read it in Welsh . . . the oldest things . . .

He took his glasses from his shirt pocket, as if fiddling with them could clear his mind, and he saw staring up out of them the reflection of his own eyes. Strange eyes . . . creepy eyes, they called them at school. At school. At school . . . Strange round tawny eyes, like the eyes of an owl. He put the glasses slowly back in his pocket, his mind groping at an echo. At his side, Cafall shifted very slightly, his head moving so that it touched Bran's hand. The fur brushed his fingers lightly, very lightly, like the flick of feathers. Feathers. Feathers. *Feathers* . . .

He had it.

Will, at his side, felt in his own mind the echoing flood of relief, and struggled to contain his delight.

Bran stood up straight and cleared his throat. "The Three Elders of the World," he said, "are the Owl of Cwm Cawlwyd, the Eagle of Gwernabwy, and the Blackbird of Celli Gadarn."

Will said softly, "Oh, well done! Well done!"

"That is right," said the thin voice above them, unemotionally. Like an early-morning sky the light blue robe swirled before them, and the figure sank back into its throne.

From the central throne rose the lord in the sea-blue robe; stepping forward, he looked down at Will. Behind its grey beard his face seemed oddly young, though its skin was brown and weathered like the skin off a sailor long at sea.

"Will Stanton," he said, "who were the three generous men of the Island of Britain?"

Will stared at him. The riddle was not impossible; he knew that the answer lay somewhere in his memory, stored from the great Book of Gramarye, treasure book of the enchantment of the Light that had been destroyed as soon as he, the last of the Old Ones, had been shown what it held. Will set his mind to work, searching. But at the same time a deeper riddle worried at him. Who was this lord in the sea-blue robe, with his close interest in Bran? He knew about Cafall . . . clearly he was a lord of the High Magic, and yet there was a look about him of . . . a look of . . .

Will pushed the wondering aside. The answer to the riddle had surfaced in his memory.

He said clearly, "The three generous men of the Island of Britain. Nudd the Generous, son of Senllyt. Mordaf the Generous, son of Serwan. Rhydderch the Generous, son of Tydwal Tudglyd. *And Arthur himself was more generous than the three.*"

Deliberately on the last line his voice rang echoing through the hall like a bell.

"That is right," said the bearded lord. He looked thoughtfully at Will and seemed about to say more, but instead he only nodded slowly. Then sweeping his robe about him in a sea-blue wave, he stepped back to his throne.

The hall seemed darker, filled with dancing shadows from the flickering light of the fire. A sudden flash and crackle came from behind the boys, as a log fell and the flames leapt up; instinctively Will glanced back. When he turned forward again, the third figure, who had not spoken or moved until now, was standing tall and silent before his throne. His robe was a deep, deep blue, darkest of the three, and his hood was pulled so far forward that there was no hint of his face visible, but only shadow.

His voice was deep and resonant, like the voice of a cello, and it brought music into the hall.

"Will Stanton," it said, "what is the shore that fears the sea?"

Will started impulsively forward, his hands clenching into fists, for this voice caught into the deepest part of him. Surely, surely . . . but the face in the hood was hidden, and he was denied all ways of recognition. Any part of his senses that tried to reach out to the great thrones met a blank wall of refusal from the High Magic. Once more Will gave up, and put his mind to the last riddle.

He said slowly, "The shore that fears the sea . . ."

Images wavered in and out of his mind: great crashing waves against a rocky coast . . . the green light in the ocean, the realm of Tethys, where strange creatures may live . . . a gentler sea then, washing in long slow waves an endless golden beach. The shore . . . the beach . . . the beach . . .

The image wavered and changed. It dissolved into a green dappled forest of gnarled ancient trees, their broad trunks smooth with a curious light grey bark. Their leaves danced above, new, soft, bright with a delicate green that had in it all of springtime. The beginnings of triumph whispered in Will's mind.

"The shore," he said. "The beach where the sea washes. But also it is a wood, of lovely fine grain, that is in the handle of a chisel and the legs of a chair, the head of a broom and the pad of a work-horse saddle. And I dare swear too that those two chests between your thrones are carved of it. The only places where it may not be used are beneath the open sky and upon the open sea, for this wood loses its virtue if soaked by water. The answer to your riddle, my lord, is the wood of the beech tree."

The flames leaped up in the fire behind them, and suddenly the hall was brilliant. Joy and relief seemed to surge through the air. The first two blue-robed lords rose from their thrones to stand beside the third; like three towers they loomed hooded over the boys. Then the third lord flung back the hood of his deep blue robe, to reveal a fierce hawk-nosed head with deep-set eyes and a shock of wild white hair. And the high Magic's barrier against recognition fell away.

Will cried joyously, "Merriman!"

He leapt forward to the tall figure as a small child leaps to its father, and clasped his outstretched hands. Merriman smiled down at him.

Will laughed aloud in delight. "I knew," he said. "I knew. And yet —"

"Greetings, Old One." Merriman said. "Now you are grown fully into the Circle, by this. Had you failed in this part of the quest, all else would have been lost." The bleak, hard lines of his face were softened by affection; his dark eyes blazed like black torches. Then he turned to Bran, taking him by the shoulders. Bran looked up at him, pale and expressionless.

"And the raven boy," the deep voice said gently. "We meet again. You have played your part well, as it was known you would. Hold your head in pride, Bran Davies. You carry a great heritage within you. Much has been asked of you, and more will be asked yet. Much more."

Bran looked at Merriman with his catlike eyes unblinking, and said nothing. Listening to the Welsh boy's mood, Will sensed an uneasy baffled pleasure.

Merriman stepped back. He said, "Three Lords of the High Magic have for many centuries had guardianship of the golden harp. There are no names here in this place, nor allegiances in that task. Here, as in other places that you do not know yet, all is subject to the law, the High Law. It is of no consequence that I am a Lord of the Light, or that my colleague there is a Lord of the Dark."

He made a slight ironic bow to the tall figure who wore the robe of lightest blue. Will caught his breath in sudden comprehension, and looked for the thin face hidden in the hood. But it was turned away from him, staring out into the shadows of the hall.

The central figure in the sea-blue robe stepped forward a pace. There was great quiet authority about him, as if he were confident, without pomp, in knowing himself the master in that hall. He put back his hood and they saw the full strength and gentleness of the close-bearded face. Though his beard was grey, his hair was brown, only lightly grey-streaked. He seemed a man in the middle of his years, with all power undiminished, yet wisdom already gained. *But*, Will thought, *he is not a man at all* . . .

Merriman inclined his head respectfully, stepping aside. "Sire," he said.

105

Will stared, at last beginning to understand.

At Bran's side, the dog Cafall made the same small sound of devotion that he had before. Clear blue eyes looked down at Bran, and the bearded lord said softly, "Fortune guard you in my land, my son."

Then as Bran looked at him perplexed, the lord drew himself up, and his voice rose. "Will Stanton," he said. "Two chests stand between our thrones. You must open the chest at my right, and take out what you will find there. The other will remain sealed, in case of need, until another time that I hope may never come. Here now."

He turned, pointing. Will went to the big carved chest, turned its ornate wrought-iron clasp, and pushed at the top. It was so broad, and the carved slab of wood so heavy, that he had to kneel and push upward with all the force of both arms; but he shook his head in warning refusal when Bran started forward to help.

Slowly the huge lid rose, and fell open, and for a moment there was a delicate sound like singing in the air. Then Will reached inside the chest, and when he straightened again he was bearing in both his arms a small, gleaming, golden harp.

The hint of music in the hall died into nothing, giving way to a low growing rumble like distant thunder. Closer and louder it grew. The lord in the lightest, sky-blue robe, his face still hooded and hidden, drew away from them. He seized his cloak and swung it round with a long sweep of the arm.

106

The fire hissed and went out. Smoke filled the hall, dark and bitter. Thunder crashed and roared all around. And the lord in the sky-blue robe gave a great cry of rage, and disappeared.

Eyes That See The
Wind

They stood silent in the dim-lit darkness. Somewhere out beyond the rock, thunder still rumbled and growled. The torches burned, flickering and smoky, on the walls.

Bran said huskily: "Was he the — the —"

"No," Merriman said. "He is not the Grey King. But he is one very close to him, and back to him he has now gone. And their rage will mount the higher because it will be sharpened by fear, fear at what the Light may be able to do with this new Thing of Power." He looked at Will, his bony face tight with concern. "The first perilous part of the quest is accomplished, Old One, but there is worse peril yet to come."

"The Sleepers must be wakened," Will said.

"That is right. And although we do not yet know where they sleep, nor shall till you have found them, it is almost certain that they are terribly, dangerously close to the Grey King. For long we have known there was a reason for his hard cold grip on this part of the land, though we did not understand it. A happy valley, this has always been, and beautiful; yet he chose to make his kingdom here, instead of in some grim remote place of the kind chosen by most of his line. Now it is clear there can be only one reason for that: to be close to the place where the Sleepers lie, and to keep their resting-place within his power. Just as this great rock, Craig yr Aderyn, is still within his power . . ."

Will said, his round face grave, "The spell of protection, by which we came here untouched, has run its course now. And it can be made only once." He looked ruefully at Bran. "We may have an interesting reception out there, when we leave this place."

"Have no care, Old One. You will have a new protection with you now."

The words came deep and gentle from the top of the hall. Turning, Will saw that the bearded lord, his robe blue as the summer sea, was sitting enthroned again in the shadows. As he spoke, it seemed that the light began gradually to grow in the hall; the torches burned higher, and glimmering between them now Will could see long swords hanging on the stone.

"The music of the golden harp," said the blue-robed lord, "has a power that may not be broken either by the Dark or by the Light. It has the High Magic in it, and while the harp is being played, those under its protection are safe from any kind of harm or spell. Play the harp of gold, Old One. Its music will wrap you in safety."

Will said slowly, "By enchantment I could play it, but I think it should rather be played by the art of skilful fingers. I do not know how to play the harp, my lord." He paused. "But Bran does."

Bran looked down at the instrument as Will held it out to him.

"Never a harp like that, though," he said.

He took the harp from Will. Its frame was slender but ornate, fashioned so that a golden vine with gold leaves and flowers seemed to twine round it, in and out of the strings. Even the strings themselves looked as if they were made of gold.

"Play, Bran," said the bearded lord softly.

Holding the harp experimentally in the crook of his left arm, Bran ran his fingers gently over the strings. And the sounds that came from them were of such sweetness that Will, beside him, caught his breath in astonishment; he had never heard notes at once so delicate and so resonant, filling the hall with music like the liquid birdsong of summer. Intent, fascinated, Bran began to pick out the plaintive notes of an old Welsh lullaby, elaborating it gradually, filling it out, as he gained confidence in the feel of the strings under his one hand. Will watched the absorbed musician's devotion on his face. Glancing for an instant at the enthroned lord, and at Merriman, he knew that they too were for this moment rapt, carried away out of time by a music that was not of the earth, pouring out like the High Magic in a singing spell.

Cafall made no sound, but leaned his head against Bran's knee.

Merriman said, his deep voice soft over the music, "Go now, Old One." His shadowed, deep-set eyes met Will's briefly, in a fierce communication of trust and hope. Will stared about him for a last moment at the high torchlit hall, with its one dark-robed figure standing tall as a tree, and the unknown bearded lord seated motionless on his throne. Then he turned and led Bran, his fingers still gently plucking a melody from the harp, towards the narrow stone staircase to the chamber from which they had come. When he had set him climbing, he turned to raise one arm in salute, then followed.

Bran stood in the stone room above, playing, while Cafall and Will came up after him. And as he played, there took shape in the blank wall at the end of the chamber, below the single hanging golden shield, the two great doors through which they had come into the heart of Bird Rock.

The music of the harp rippled in a lilting upward scale, and slowly the doors swung inward. Beyond, they saw the grey, cloudy sky between the steep walls of the cleft of rock. Though fire blazed no longer on the mountain, a strong, dead smell of burning hung in the air. As they stepped outside, Cafall bounded out past them, through the cleft, and disappeared.

Struck suddenly by a fear of losing him again, Bran stopped playing. "Cafall! Cafall!" he called.

"Look!" Will said softly.

He was half-turned, looking back. Behind them, the tall slabs of rock swung silently together and seemed to melt out of existence, leaving only a weathered rock face, looking just as it had looked for thousands of years. And in the air hung a faint vanishing phrase of delicate music. But Bran was thinking only of Cafall. After one brief glance at the rock, he tucked the harp beneath his arm and dived for the opening through which the dog had disappeared.

Before he could reach it, a whirling flurry of white came hurling in upon them through a cloud of fine ash, snarling, kicking, knocking Bran sideways so hard that he almost dropped the harp. It was Cafall; but a mad, furious, transformed Cafall, growling at them, glaring, driving them deeper into the cleft as if they were enemies. In a moment or two he had them pinned astounded against the rocky wall, and was crouching before them with his long side-teeth bared in a cold snarl.

"What is it?" said Bran blankly when he had breath enough to speak. "Cafall? What on earth —"

And in an instant they knew — or would have known, if they had had time still for wondering. For suddenly the whole world round them was a roaring flurry of noise and destruction. Broken, charred branches came whirling past over the top of the rocky cleft; stones came bounding down loose out of nowhere so that instinctively they ducked, covering their heads. They fell flat on the ground, pressing themselves into the angle between earth and rock, with Cafall close beside. All around, the wind howled and tore at the rock with a sound like a high mad human scream amplified beyond belief. It was as if all the air in Wales had funnelled down into a great tornado of tearing destruction, and was battering in a frenzy of frustrated rage at the narrow opening in whose shelter they desperately crouched.

Will lurched up on to his hands and knees. He groped with one hand until he clutched Bran's arm. "The harp!" he croaked. "Play the harp!"

Bran blinked at him, dazed by the noise overhead, and then he understood. Forcing himself up against the fearsome wind pressing in between the rocky walls, he gripped the golden harp against his side and ran his right hand tremulously over the strings.

At once the tumult grew less. Bran began to play, and as the sweet notes poured out like the song of a lark rising, the great wind died away into nothing. Outside, there was only the rattle of loose pebbles tumbling here and there, one by one, down the rock. For a moment a lone sunbeam slanted down and glinted on the gold of the harp. Then it was gone, and the sky seemed duller, the world more grey. Cafall scrambled to his feet, licked Bran's hand, and led them docilely out to the slope outside the narrow cleft that had sheltered them from the fury of the gale. They felt a soft rain beginning to fall.

Bran let his fingers wander idly but persistently over the strings of the harp. He had no intention of stopping again. He looked at Will, and shook his head mutely with wonder and remorse and inquiry all in one.

Will squatted down and took Cafall's muzzle between his hands. He shook the dog's head gently from side to side. "Cafall! Cafall!" he said wonderingly. Over his shoulder he said to Bran, "*Gwynt Traed y Meirw*, is that how you say it? In all its ancient force the Grey King sent his north wind upon us, the wind that blows round the feet of the dead, and with the dead is where we should have been if it weren't for Cafall — blasted away into a time beyond tomorrow. Before we could have seen a single tree bending, it would have been on us, for it came down from very high up and no human sighted eye could have seen it. But this hound of yours is the dog with the silver eyes, and such dogs can see the wind . . . So he saw it, and knew what it would do, and drove us back into safety."

Bran said guiltily, "If I hadn't stopped playing, perhaps the Brenin Llwyd couldn't even have sent the wind. The magic of the harp would have stopped him."

"Perhaps," Will said. "And perhaps not." He gave Cafall's head one last rub and straightened up. The white sheepdog looked up at Bran, tongue lolling as if in a grin, and Bran said to him lovingly, "*Rwyt ti'n gi doa.* Good boy." But still his fingers did not stop moving over the harp.

114

Slowly they scrambled down the rock. Though it was full morning now, the sky was no lighter, but grey and heavy with cloud; the rain was still light, but it was clear that it would grow and settle in for the day, and that the valley was safe now from any more threat of fire. All the near slope of the mountain, Bird Rock and the valley edge were blackened and charred, and here and there wisps of smoke still rose. But all sparks were drowned now, and the ashes cold and wet, and the green farmlands would not again this year be in any state for burning.

Bran said, "Did the harp bring the rain?"

"I think so," Will said. "I am just hoping it will bring nothing else. That's the trouble with the High Magic, like talking in the Old Speech — it's a protection, and yet it marks you, makes you easy to find."

"We'll be in the valley soon." But as he spoke, Bran's foot slipped on a wet rock face and he stumbled sideways, grabbing at a bush to save himself from falling — and dropped the harp. In the instant that the music broke off, Cafall's head jerked up and he began barking furiously, in a mixture of rage and challenge. He jumped up on to a projecting rock and stood poised there, staring about him. Then suddenly the barking broke into a furious deep howl, like the baying of a hunting dog, and he leapt.

The great grey fox, king of the *milgwn*, swerved in mid-air and screamed like a vixen. In a headlong rush down Bird Rock he had sprung out at them from above, aiming straight for Bran's head and neck. But the shock of Cafall's fierce leap turned his balance just enough to send him spinning sideways, cartwheeling down the rock. He screamed again, an unnatural sound that made the boys flinch in horror, and did not stop himself to turn at bay, but rushed on in a frenzy down the mountain. In an instant Cafall, barking in joyous triumph, was tearing down after him.

And Will, up on the empty rock under the grey drizzling sky, was instantly filled with a presentiment of disaster so overpowering that without thought he reached out and seized the golden harp, and cried to Bran, "Stop Cafall! Stop him! Stop him!"

Bran gave him one frightened look. Then he flung himself after Cafall, running, stumbling, desperately calling the dog back. Scrambling down from the rock with the harp under one arm, Will saw his white head moving fast over the nearest field and, beyond it, a blur of speed that he knew was Cafall pursuing the grey fox. His head dizzy with foreboding, he too ran. Still on high land, he could see two fields away the roofs of Caradog Prichard's farm, and near by a grey-white knot of sheep and the figures of men. He skidded to a halt suddenly. The harp! There was no means of explaining the harp, if anyone should see it. He was certain to be among men in a few moments. The harp must be hidden. But where?

He looked wildly about him. The fire had not touched this field. On the far side of the field he saw a small lean-to, no more than three stone walls and a slate roof, that was an open shelter for sheep in winter, or a storeplace for winter feed. It was filled with bales of hay already, newly stacked. Running to it, Will thrust the gleaming little harp between two bales of hay, so that it was completely invisible from the outside. Then standing back, he stretched out one hand, and in the Old Speech put upon the harp the Spell of Caer Garadawg, by the power of which only the song of an Old One would be able to take the harp out of that place, or even make it visible at all.

Then he rushed away over the field towards Prichard's Farm, where distant shouts marked the ending of the chase. He could see, in a meadow beyond the farm buildings, the huge grey fox swerving and leaping in an effort to shake Cafall from its heels, and Cafall running doggedly close. A madness seemed to be on the fox; white foam dripped from its jaws. Will stumbled breathless into the farmyard to find Bran struggling to make his way through a group of men and sheep at the gate. John Rowlands was there, and Owen Davies, with Will's uncle; their clothes and weary faces were still blackened with ash from the fire-fighting, and Caradog Prichard stood scowling with his gun cocked under his arm.

"That damn dog has gone mad!" Prichard growled.

"Cafall! Cafall!" Bran pushed his way wildly through into the field, scattering the sheep, paying no heed to anyone. Prichard snarled at him, and Owen Davies said sharply, "Bran! Where have you been? What are you up to?"

The grey fox leapt high in the air, as they had seen it do once before on Bird Rock. Cafall leapt after it, snapping at it in mid-air.

"The dog is mad," David Evans said unhappily. "He will be on the sheep —"

"He's just so determined to get that fox!" Bran's voice was high with anguish. "Cafall! *Tyrd yma!* Leave it!"

Will's uncle looked at Bran as if he could not believe what he had heard. Then he looked down at Will. He said, puzzled, "*What fox?*"

Horror exploded in Will's brain, as suddenly he understood, and he cried out. But it was too late. The grey fox in the field swung about and came leaping straight at them, with Cafall at his heels. At the last moment it curved sideways and leapt at one of the sheep that now milled terrified round the gate, and sank its teeth into the woolly throat. The sheep screamed. Cafall sprang at the fox. Twenty yards away, Caradog Prichard let out a great furious shout, lifted his gun, and shot Cafall full in the chest.

"Cafall!" Bran's cry of loving horror struck at Will so that for a second he closed his eyes in pain; he knew that the grief in it would ring in his ears for ever.

The grey fox stood waiting for Will to look at it, grinning, red tongue lolling from a mouth dripping brighter with red blood. It stared straight at him with an unmistakable sneering snarl. Then it loped off across the field, straight as an arrow, and disappeared over the far hedge.

Bran was on his knees by the dog, sobbing, cradling the white head on his lap. He called desperately to Cafall, fondling his ears, dropping his cheek just once, in longing, to rest against the smooth neck. But there was nothing to be done. The chest was a shattered ruin. The silver eyes were glazed, unblinking. Cafall was dead.

"Murdering bloody dog!" Prichard was babbling with fury still, in a kind of savage contentment. "He'll kill no more of my sheep! A damn good riddance!"

"He was just after the fox. He was trying to save your old sheep!" Bran choked on his words, and wept.

"What are you talking about? A fox? *Dammo*, boy, you are as mad as the dog." Prichard broke the shell out of his gun, his pudgy face contemptuous.

Owen Davies was down on his knees beside Bran. "Come, *bachgen*," he said, his voice gentle. "There was no fox anywhere. Cafall was going for the sheep, there is no question. We all saw. He was a lovely dog, a beauty" — his voice shook, and he cleared his throat — "but he must have gone bad in the head. I cannot say that I would not have shot him myself, in Caradog's place. That is the right of it. Once a dog turns killer, it is the only thing to do."

His arm was tight round Bran's shoulders. Bran looked up at the rest of them, blindly tugging off his glasses and rubbing a hand over his eyes. He said, high, incredulous, "But did none of you see the fox? The big grey fox that Cafall jumped as it went to kill the sheep?"

John Rowlands said, his voice deep and compassionate, "No, Bran."

"There was no fox, Bran," David Evans said. "I'm sorry, boy *bach*. Come on, now. Let your father take you to Clwyd. We will bring Cafall after you."

"Ah," said Prichard with a sniff. "You can get that carrion out of my yard as soon as you like, yes. And pay the vet's bill when I have had that sheep seen to, as well."

"*Cae dy geg*, Caradog Prichard," said Will's uncle sharply. "There will be talk of all this sheep attacking business later. You can have a little feeling for the boy, surely."

Caradog Prichard looked at him, his small eyes bright and expressionless. He motioned to one of his men to take the wounded sheep away. Then he spat, casually, on the ground, and walked off to his farmhouse. A woman was standing there in the doorway. She had not moved through everything that had happened.

Bran's father helped him to his feet, and led him away. Bran seemed dazed. He looked at Will blankly, as if he had not been there.

David Evans said glumly, "Wait a minute. There is some sacking in the car. I will come and find it."

John Rowlands stood beside Will in the fine rain, sucking at an empty pipe, looking reflectively down at the still white body with the dreadful red gash in its chest. He said, "And did you see this fox, Will Stanton?"

"Yes," Will said. "Of course. It was in front of us as clear as you are now. It had tried to attack us on Bird Rock, and Cafall chased it down here. But none of you could see it. So nobody will ever believe us, will they?"

John Rowlands was silent for a moment, his creased brown face unreadable. Then he said, "Sometimes in these mountains there are things it is very hard to believe, even when you have seen them with your own eyes. For instance, there is Cafall, and with our eyes we saw him alone jump at that sheep. And indeed something did sink its teeth into the sheep's throat and must have got a bloody mouth doing it, for there was blood all over the sheep's fleece and it is lucky to be alive. And yet it is a strange thing, which will not go out of my mind — that although poor Cafall lies there with his own blood all over his broken chest, *there is no blood on his mouth at all.*"

PART TWO

THE SLEEPERS

THE GIRL FROM THE MOUNTAINS

Will said, "Excuse me, Mr Davies, is Bran home from school yet?"

Owen Davies jerked upright. He had been bent over the engine of a tractor in one of the farm outhouses; his thin hair was ruffled and his face smeared with oil.

"I'm sorry," Will said. "I made you jump."

"No, no, boy, that is all right. I was just a bit further away than this engine, I think . . ." He made the quick apologetic grimace that seemed to be as near as he ever came to a smile. All the lines on his thin face seemed to lead nowhere, Will thought: no expression, ever. "Bran is home, yes. I think you will find him in the house. Or up by . . ." His light, worried voice trailed away.

Will said softly, "By Cafall." They had buried the dog the evening before, up on the lower slope of the mountain, with a heavy stone over the grave to keep predators away.

"Yes, I think so. Up there," Owen Davies said.

Will wanted suddenly to say something, but the words were slippery. "Mr Davies, I'm sorry about that. All of it. Yesterday. It was awful."

"Well, yes now, thank you." Owen Davies was embarrassed, flinching from the contact of emotion. He said, looking down into the tractor's engine, "It couldn't be helped. You can never tell when a dog may take it into his head to go for the sheep. It is one in a million, but it can happen. Even the best dog in the world . . ." He looked up suddenly, and for once his eyes met Will's, though they seemed to be looking not at him but beyond, into the future or the past. His voice came firmer, like that of a younger man. "I do think, mind you, that Caradog Prichard was very ready to shoot the dog. That is something very drastic, and not done normally to another man's creature, at any rate not before his face. We were all there, it would have been nothing to catch Cafall. And a sheep-chaser can sometimes be given a home, somewhere away from sheep, without having to be killed . . . But I cannot say this to Bran, and nor must you either. It would not help him."

His eyes flicked away again, and Will watched, fascinated and disturbed, as the bright echo of another time dropped away like a coat and left the familiar drab Owen Davies with his humourless, slightly guilty air.

"Well," Will said. "I think you are right, but no, I wouldn't mention that to Bran. I'll go and look for him now."

"Yes," Owen Davies said eagerly, turning his anxious, helpless face to the hills. "Yes, you could help him, I believe."

But Will knew, as he trudged along the muddy lane, that there was small chance he, or anyone of the Light, could comfort Bran.

When he reached the edge of the valley, where the land began to climb, he saw very small and distant above him, halfway up the mountain, the figure of John Rowlands like a toy man. His two dogs, black-and-white specks, moved to and fro. Will looked, irresolute, at the place further down the valley where Bran would be gone to earth: alone with his misery. Then on an instinct he began to climb straight up, through the bracken and gorse. John Rowlands might be a good person to talk to, first.

Nevertheless it was Bran he first saw,

He came upon him suddenly, without expecting it. He was partway up the slope, panting hard as he still did on rising ground, and as he paused for breath, raising his head, he saw there before him sitting on a rock the familiar figure: dark jeans and sweater, white hair like a beacon, smoky glasses over the pale eyes. But the glasses were not visible now, nor the eyes, for Bran sat with his head bent down, immobile, even though Will knew he must have heard the noisy puffing of his approach.

He said, "Hallo, Bran."

Bran raised his head slowly, but said nothing.

Will said, "There was no dog like him, ever, anywhere."

"No, there was not," Bran said. His voice was small and husky; he sounded tired.

Will cast about to find words of comfort, but his mind could not help but use the wisdom of an Old One, and that was not the way to reach Bran. He said, "It was a man that killed him, Bran, but that is the price we have to pay for the freedom of men on the earth. That they can do the bad things as well as the good. There are shadows in the pattern, as well as sunlight. Just as you once told me, Cafall was no ordinary dog. He was a part of the long pattern, like the stars and the sea. And nobody could have played his part better, nobody in the whole world."

The valley was quiet under its brooding grey sky; Will heard only a song thrush trifling from a tree, the scattered voices of sheep on the slopes; the faint humming, from the distant road, of a passing car.

Bran raised his head and took off his glasses; the tawny eyes were swollen and red-rimmed in his white face. He sat there hunched, knees bent up, arms dangling limp over them.

"Go away," he said. "Go away. I wish you had never come here. I wish I had never heard of the Light and the Dark, and your damned old Merriman and his rhymes. If I had your golden harp now I would throw it in the sea. I am not a part of your stupid quest any more, I don't care what happens to it. And Cafall was never a part of it either, or a part of your pretty pattern. He was my dog, and I loved him more than anything in the world, and now he is dead. *Go away*."

The red-rimmed eyes stared cold and unwinking at Will for a long moment, and then Bran put back his smoky glasses and turned his head to look out across the valley. It was a dismissal. Without a word, Will stood straight again and plodded on up the hill.

It seemed a long time before he reached John Rowlands. The lean, leathery sheepman was crouched half-kneeling over a broken fence, mending it from a prickly skein of barbed wire. He sat back on his heels as Will came panting up, and looked at him through narrowed eyes, his seamed brown face crinkled against the brightness of the sky. With no greeting, he said, "This is the top level of the Clwyd pasture here. The hill farms have the grazing beyond — the fence is to keep our sheep below. But they are crafty beggars at breaking it, especially now the rams are out."

Will nodded, miserably.

John Rowlands looked at him for a moment, then got up and beckoned him over to a high outcropping of rock a little way up the mountain. They sat down on its lee side; even there the place was like a lookout post, governing the whole valley. Will glanced round him briefly, his senses alert, but the Grey King still lay withdrawn; the valley was as quiescent as it had been since the moment Cafall had died.

John Rowlands said, "There is the rest of the fence to check, but I am ready for a break. I have a thermos here. Would you like a mouthful of tea, Will?"

He gave him the thermos top brimming with bitter brown tea. Will surprised himself by drinking thirstily. When he had finished, John Rowlands said softly, "Did you know you were sitting near Cadfan's Way, here?"

Will looked at him sharply, and it was not the look of an eleven-year-old and he did not trouble to disguise the fact. "Yes," he said. "Of course I did. And you knew that I knew, and that's why you mentioned it."

John Rowlands sighed and poured himself some tea. "I dare say," he said in a curious tone that had envy in it, "that you could now walk blindfold all the way from Tywyn to Machynlleth over the hills on Cadfan's Way, even though you have never been to this country before."

Will pushed back his straight brown hair, damp on his forehead from the climbing. "The Old Ways are all over Britain," he said, "and we can follow one anywhere, once we have found it. Yes." He looked out across the valley. "It was Bran's dog who found it for me up here, in the beginning," he said sadly.

John Rowlands pushed back his cloth cap, scratched his head and pulled it forward again. "I have heard of you people," he said. "All my life, on and off, though not so much these days. More when I was a boy. I even used to think I'd met one of you, once, when I was very young, though I dare say it

was only a dream . . . And now I have been thinking
about the way the dog died, and I have talked a bit
to young Bran."

He broke off, and Will looked nervously to see
what he might say next, but did not choose to use
his art to find out.

"And I think, Will Stanton," said the sheepman,
"that I ought to be helping you in any way that you
might need. But I do not want to know what you
are doing, I do not want you to explain it to me at
all."

Will felt suddenly as if the sun had burst out.
"Thank you," he said. The smaller of John Rowlands's dogs, Tip, came quietly over and sat down
at his feet, and he rubbed the silky ears.

John Rowlands looked down over the bracken-
brown slope; Will's gaze followed his. Just above
the blackened land where the fire had grazed, they
could see the tiny figure that was Bran, sitting
hunched with his back to them, his white head
propped on his knees.

"This is a very bad time for Bran Davies," the
shepherd said.

"I'm glad he talked to you," Will said bleakly.
"He wouldn't talk to me. Not that I blame him.
He'll be so lonely, without Cafall. I mean, Mr
Davies is nice, but not exactly . . . and not having
any mother, too, that makes it worse."

"Bran never knew his mother," John Rowlands
said. "He was too small."

Will said curiously, "What was she like?"

Rowlands drank his tea, shook the cup dry and screwed it back on the flask.

"Her name was Gwen," he said. He held the flask absentmindedly in his hands, looking past it into his memory. "She was one of the prettiest things you will ever see. Small, with a clear fair skin and black hair, and blue eyes like speedwell, and a smiling light in her face that was like music. But she was a strange wild girl too. Out of the mountains she came, and never would tell where she came from, or how . . ."

He turned abruptly and looked hard at Will, with the dark eyes that seemed always to be narrowed against fierce weather. "I should have thought," he said with sudden belligerence, "that being what you are, you would know all about Bran."

Will said gently, "I don't know anything about Bran, except what he has told me. We are not really so very different from you, Mr Rowlands, most of us. Only our masters are different. We do know many things, but they are not things that intrude on the lives of men. In that, we are like anyone else — we know only what we have lived through, or what somebody has told us."

John Rowlands nodded his head, relenting. He opened his mouth to say something, stopped, pulled his pipe from his pocket and poked at its contents with one finger. "Well," he said slowly, "perhaps I should tell you the story from the start. It will help you to understand Bran. He knows some of it well enough himself — indeed he thinks about it so

130

much, on his own, that I wish he had never been told."

Will said nothing. He sat closer to Tip, and put one arm round his neck.

John Rowlands lit his pipe. He said, through the first cloud of smoke, "It was when Owen Davies was a young man, working at Prichard's Farm. Old Mr Prichard was alive in those days. Caradog worked for his father too, waiting to take over and run the place, though he wasn't a patch on Owen for work ... Owen was sheepman for Prichard. A solitary chap he was, even then. He was living in a cottage on his own. Out on the moor, closer to the sheep than to the farm." He puffed out some more smoke, and glanced at Will. "You have been at that cottage. It is deserted now. Nobody has lived there for years."

"That place? Where you left the sheep, after —" Startled, Will saw again in his mind the figure of John Rowlands staggering into the little empty stone house in the bracken, with the wounded sheep draped over his shoulders and blood from its fleece on his neck. The little house from which, when they had come back half an hour later, the hurt sheep had vanished without any trace.

"That place. Yes. And one wild night in the winter, with rain and a north wind blowing, there was a knocking at Owen's door. It was a girl, out of nowhere, half-frozen with walking through the storm. And worn out from carrying her baby."

"Her baby?"

John Rowlands looked down the mountain at Bran's hunched figure, sitting lonely on his rock. "A sturdy little chap the baby was, just a few months old. She had him in a kind of sling on her back. The only strange thing about him, Owen saw, was that he had no colour in him. White face, white hair, white eyebrows, and very odd tawny eyes like the eyes of an owl . . ."

Will said slowly, "I see."

"Owen took the girl in," John Rowlands said. "He got her back to life, gradually, with much care, that night and the day after — and the baby too, though babies are tough creatures and he was not in such a bad way. And before twenty-four hours were even gone, Owen Davies was more in love with that strange beautiful girl than I have ever seen a man love a woman. He had never loved anyone much before. Very shy, was Owen. It was like a dam bursting . . . With a man like that, it is dangerous — when at last he loves, he gives all his heart without care or thinking, and it may never go back to him for the rest of his life." He stopped for a moment, compassion softening his weatherlined face, and sat in silence. Then he said, "Well. There they were, then. The next day Owen went off to the sheep, leaving the girl to rest in the cottage. On the way home he stopped at my house, on Clwyd here, to get some milk for the baby. We had always been friends since he was a boy, even though I am older. I was not there, but my wife was, and he told her about Gwen and the baby. My Blodwen has a warm heart and a good ear. She said he was like a man on fire, glowing, he had to tell somebody . . ."

Far down on the lower slope, Bran got up from his rock and began roaming aimlessly through the bracken, peering about as though he were looking for something.

"When Owen came back to his cottage," John Rowlands said, "he heard screaming. He had never heard a woman scream before. There was a strange dog outside the door. Caradog Prichard's dog. Owen went into the house like a wire snapping, and he found the girl struggling with Caradog. He had come looking to see why Owen had not been at work the day before, had Caradog, and found Gwen there instead, and decided in his dirty way that she must be a light woman, and easy for him to take if he fancied her . . ." John Rowlands leaned deliberately to one side and spat into the grass. "Excuse me, Will," he said, "but that is how I feel when my mouth has been talking about Caradog Prichard."

"What happened? What did he do?" Will was lost in wonder at this mist of romance surrounding him, ordinary Owen Davies.

"Owen? He went mad. He has never been a fighter, but he threw Caradog out of the door, and went after him, and he broke his nose and knocked out two of his teeth. Then I arrived, and a good thing I did or he would have killed the man. Blodwen had sent me with some things for the baby. I took Caradog home. He wouldn't have the doctor called. Afraid of the scandal, he was. I cannot say I had very much sympathy for him. His nose has not looked quite the same shape since."

He glanced down the slope again. Bran's white head was still bent over the ground, as he moved slowly, meaninglessly to and fro.

"Bran may be glad of your company soon, Will. There is not much more to tell, really. One more day and one more night the girl Gwen stayed with Owen in the cottage, and he asked her to marry him. He was such a happy man, the light shone out of him. We saw them for part of that day, and she seemed just as joyful too. But then, just about dawn on the next morning, the fourth day, Owen was wakened by the baby's crying, and Gwen was not there. She had vanished. No one knew where she had gone. And she never came back."

Will said, "Bran told me she died."

"Bran knows she disappeared," John Rowlands said. "But perhaps it is more comfortable to believe that your mother died than to think of her running away and leaving you without a second thought."

"That's what she did? Just disappeared and left the baby behind?"

John Rowlands nodded. "And a note. It said: *His name is Bran. Thank you, Owen Davies*. And that was all. Wherever she went, she has never been seen or heard of since, nor will she ever be. Owen came to us with the baby that morning. He was out of his head, crazy with losing Gwen. He went up into the hills, and did not come down for three days. Looking for her, you see. People heard him

134

calling, *Gwennie, Gwennie* ... Blodwen and Mrs
Evans, your auntie, looked after Bran between them.
A good baby, he was ... Old man Prichard gave
Owen the sack, of course. About that time your
uncle David lost a man, so he took Owen on, and
Owen moved to the cottage on Clwyd where he
lives now."

"And he brought Bran up as his son," Will said.

"That's right. With everybody's help. There was
a bit of a to-do, but he was allowed to adopt the boy
in the end. Most people ended up thinking Bran
really was Owen's son. And the one thing that Bran
has never been told is that he is not — he believes
that Owen is his father, and you must take care you
never suggest anything different."

"I shall," Will said.

"Yes. I have no worries about you ... Sometimes
I think Owen believes Bran is his real son too. He
was always strict chapel, you see, and afterwards he
turned even more to his religion. Perhaps you
cannot understand this quite, Will *bach*, but because
Owen knew it was wrong by the rules of his faith
to live those few days alone in the same house with
Gwen, then he began to feel that it was just as much
wrong as if he and Gwennie, not married to each
other, had had a baby together. As if the two of
them *had* produced Bran. So when he thinks of
Bran — still, to this day — it is mostly with love,
but a little bit — with guilt. For no good reason,
mind, except in his own conscience. He has too
much conscience, has Owen. The people do not

care, even the people of his chapel — they think Bran is his natural son, but the tut-tutting was over long ago. They have brains enough to judge a man by what he has proved himself to be, not by some mistake he may or may not have made a long time ago."

John Rowlands sighed, and stretched, knocked out his pipe and ground the ashes into the earth. He stood up; the dogs jumped to his side. He looked down at Will.

"There was all this at the back," he said, "when Caradog Prichard shot Bran Davies's dog."

Will picked a single blossom from a gorse bush beside him; it shone bright yellow on his grubby hand. "People are very complicated," he said sadly.

"So they are," John Rowlands said. His voice deepened a little, louder and clearer than it had been. "But when the battles between you and your adversaries are done, Will Stanton, in the end the fate of all the world will depend on just those people, and on how many of them are good or bad, stupid or wise. And indeed it is all so complicated that I would not dare foretell what they will do with their world. Our world." He whistled softly. "*Tyrd yma*, Pen, Tip."

Carefully he picked up his loop of barbed wire, and with the dogs following, he walked away beside the fence, over the hill.

The Grey King

Will went slowly across the slope towards Bran. It was a grey day now; the rain had fallen all night, and there was more to come. The sky was lowering, ominous, and all the mountains were lost in ragged cloud. Will thought: *the breath of the Brenin Llwyd*...

He saw Bran begin climbing away up the hill, diagonally, in an obvious effort to avoid him. Will paused, and decided to give up. A ridiculous game of dodging across the mountain would do no one any good. And besides, the harp had to be taken to a safe place.

He set off through the wet bracken on the long muddy walk to the far side of Caradog Prichard's farm. His trousers were already soaked, in spite of Wellington boots borrowed from Aunt Jen. Partway, he crossed the land that had been swept by the fire, and a thin mud of black ash clung to his boots.

Will strode along moodily. He glanced round now and then in case Caradog Prichard were about, but the fields were deserted, and oddly silent. No birds sang today; even the sheep seemed quiet, and there was seldom the sound of a car drifting from the valley road. It was as if all the grey valley waited for something. Will tried to sense the mood of the place more accurately, but all the time now his mind was gradually filling again with the enmity of the Grey King, growing, growing, a whisper grown to a call, soon to grow to a furious shout. It was difficult to find attention for much else.

He came to the slate-roofed shelter where he had hidden the harp among the stacked bales of hay. The force of his own spell brought him up standing, ten feet away, as though he had walked into a glass wall.

Will smiled. Then to break the enchantment in the way appointed, he began very softly to sing. It was a spell-song of the Old Speech, and its words were not like the words of human speech, but more indefinite, a matter of nuance of sound. He was a good singer, well-taught, and the high clear notes flowed softly through the gloomy air like rays of light. Will felt the force of the resisting spell melt away. He came to the end of the verse.

Caradog Prichard's voice said coldly behind him, "Proper little nightingale, isn't it?"

Will froze. He turned slowly and stood in silence, looking at Prichard's pasty, full-cheeked face, with its crooked nose, and eyes bright as black currants.

"Well?" Prichard said impatiently. "What do you think you are doing here, standing in the middle of my field singing to the hedge? Are you mad, boy?"

138

Will gaped, changing his face subtly to an expression of total foolishness. "It was the song. I just thought of it, I wanted to try it out. They say you're a poet, you ought to understand." He let his voice drop, conspiratorially. "I write songs, sometimes, you see. But please don't tell anyone. They always laugh. They think it's stupid."

Prichard said: "Your uncle?"

"Everyone at home."

Prichard squinted at him suspiciously. The proud word "poet" had made its effect, but he was not the kind of man to relax unwarily, or for long. He said contemptuously, "Oh, the English — they know nothing of music, I am not surprised. Clods, they are. You have a very good voice, for an English boy." Then his voice sharpened suddenly. "But you weren't singing English, were you?"

"No," Will said.

"What, then?"

Will beamed at him confidentially. "Nothing, really. They were just nonsense words that seemed to go with the tune. *You* know."

But the fish did not bite. Prichard's eyes narrowed. He looked in a quick nervous movement up the valley towards the mountains, and then back at Will. He said abruptly, "I don't like you, English boy. Something funny about you, there is. All this about songs and singing does not explain why you are standing here on my land."

"Taking a short cut, that's all," Will said. "I wasn't hurting anything, honestly."

"Short cut, is it? From where to where? Your uncle's land is all over there, where you came from, and nothing is on the other side of us except moor and mountain. Nothing for you. Go back to Clwyd, nightingale, back to your snivelling little friend who lost his dog. Off. Off out of here!" All at once he was shouting, the pudgy face dusky red. "Get out! Get out!"

Will sighed. There was only one thing to be done. He had not wanted to risk attracting the closer attention of the Grey King, but it was impossible to leave the harp vulnerable to Caradog Prichard's eye. The man was glaring at him now, clenching his fists in a fit of the same unaccountable vicious rage that Will had seen overtake him before. "Get out, I tell you!"

There in the open field under the still, grey sky, Will stretched out one arm, with all five fingers stiff and pointing, and said a single quiet word. And Caradog Prichard was caught out of time, immobile, with his mouth half-open and his hand raised pointing, his face frozen in exactly the same ugly anger that had twisted it when he shot the dog Cafall. It was a pity. Will thought bitterly, that he could not be left that way forever.

But no spell lasts forever, and most for only a short breath of time. Quickly Will went forward to the stone shelter, reached in between the bales of hay, and pulled out the gleaming little golden harp. One corner of its frame was caught on an old tattered sack left among the bales; impatiently he tugged

140

both harp and sacking free, bundled them together under his arm. Then he moved round to stand behind Caradog Prichard. Once more he pointed a stiff-fingered hand at him, and spoke a single word. And Caradog Prichard, as if he had never intended to do anything else, plodded off across the field towards his farmhouse without once turning round. When he arrived there, Will knew, he would be convinced that he had gone straight home from the day's work, and he would not have an ounce of memory of Will Stanton standing in a field singing to the sky.

The plodding, paunchy form disappeared over the stile at the end of the field. Will untangled the old sack from the harp's intricate golden frame, and was about to toss it aside when he realized how useful it would be as a covering; a nameless bundle under his arm could be explained away, if he should meet someone, rather more easily than a gleaming and obviously priceless golden harp. As he slid the harp carefully inside the sack, wrinkling his nose at the hay dust puffing out, a movement across the field caught his eye. He glanced up, and for a moment even the harp left his mind.

It was the great grey fox, king of the *milgwn*, creature of the Brenin Llwyd, loping fast along the hedge. In sudden furious hatred Will flung out one pointing arm and shouted a word to stop it, and the big grey animal, no longer on its master's land, tumbled backwards in mid-stride as if it had been snatched up by a sudden tremendous high wind.

Picking itself up, it stood staring at Will, red tongue lolling. Then it lifted its long muzzle and gave one low howl, like a dog in trouble. "It's no good calling," said Will under his breath. "You can just stand there till I decide what to do with you."

But then, involuntarily, he shivered. The air seemed suddenly colder, and across the fields, all around him, he could see creeping in a low ground-mist that he had not noticed before. Slowly it came pouring over the fences, relentless, like some huge crawling creature. From every direction it came, from the mountain, the valley, the lower slopes, and when Will looked back at the grey fox standing stiff-legged in the field, he saw something else that gave a chill of new terror to the mist. The fox was changing colour. With every moment, as he watched, its sleek body and bushy tail grew darker and darker, until it became almost black.

Will stared, frowning. He thought irrelevantly, "*It looks just like Pen.*" And instantly he caught his breath, realizing something that was not irrelevant at all — that it was John Rowlands's dog Pen who, with Cafall, had been accused by Caradog Prichard of the sheep attacks made in reality by the foxes of the Grey King.

Something immeasurably strong was pushing against him, breaking his own enchantment. Whilst Will stood for a moment confused and powerless, the big fox, now black as coal, gave its strange small exultant leap into the air, grinned deliberately at him, and was off, running swiftly across the field.

It vanished through the far hedge, in the direction that Caradog Prichard had taken, towards his farm. Will knew exactly what was likely to happen when it got there, and there was nothing he could do. He was held back by the power of the Grey King, and reluctantly now he was facing an idea to which he had not given a thought before: the possibility that this power, much greater than his own, was in fact so great that he might never be able to accomplish his allotted quest.

Setting his teeth, he gripped the shrouded harp beneath his arm and set off across the field towards Clwyd Farm. Carefully he slipped under the barbed wire edging the field, crossed the corner of the next, clambered over the stile leading into the lane. But all the time his steps grew slower and slower, his breathing more laboured. Somehow, there beneath his arm, the harp was growing heavier and heavier, until he could scarcely move for the weight of it. He knew that it was not a matter of his own weakness. Against his resistance, some great enchantment was giving to the precious Thing of Power in his arm a heaviness impossible for any human strength to support. Clutching at the harp, he gasped with pain at its impossible weight, and sank down with it to the ground.

As he crouched there he raised his head and saw that the mist swirled everywhere round him now; all the world was grey-white, featureless. He stared into the mist. And gradually, the mist took shape.

The figure was so huge that at first he could not realize it was there. It stretched wider than the field, and high into the sky. It had shape, but not recognizable earthly shape; Will could see its outline from the corner of his eye, but when he looked directly at any part of it, there was nothing there. Yet there the figure loomed before him, immense and terrible, and he knew that this was a being of greater power than anything he had ever encountered in his life before. Of all the Great Lords of the Dark, none was singly more powerful and dangerous than the Grey King. But because he had remained always from the beginnings of time in his fastnesses among the Cader Idris peaks, never descending to the valleys or lower slopes, none of the Old Ones had ever encountered him, to learn what force he had at his command. So now Will, alone, last and least of the Old Ones, faced him with no defence but the inborn magic of the Light and his own wits.

A voice came from the misty shape, both sweet and terrible. It filled the air like the mist itself, and Will could not tell what language it spoke, nor whether it spoke to the hearing of the ears; he knew only that the things it said were instantly in his own mind.

"You may not wake the Sleepers, Old One," said the voice. "I will prevent you. This is my land, and in it they shall sleep forever, as they have slept these many centuries. Your harp shall not wake them. I will prevent you."

Will sat in a small crumpled heap, his arms across the harp he could no longer hold. "It is my quest," he said. "You know that I must follow it."

"Go back," said the voice, blowing through his mind like the wind. "Go back. Take the harp safely with you, a Thing of Power for the Light and your masters. I shall let you go, if you go back now and leave my land. You have won that much." The voice grew harder, more chill than the mist. "But if you seek the Sleepers, I shall destroy you, and the golden harp as well."

"No," Will said. "I am of the Light. You cannot destroy me."

"It will not differ greatly from destruction," the voice said. "Come now. You know that, Old One." It grew softer, more sibilant and nasty, as if caressing an evil thought; Will suddenly remembered the lord in the sky-blue robe.

"The powers of the Dark and the Light are equal in force, but we differ a little in our . . . treatment . . . of those we may bring under our will." The voice crawled like a slug over Will's skin. "Go back, Old One. I shall not warn the Light again."

Summoning all his confidence, Will scrambled up, leaving the harp on the ground at his feet. He made a mocking little bow to the grey mistiness that he knew, now, he must not look at directly. "You have given your warning, Majesty," he said, "and I have heard it. But it will make no difference. The Dark can never turn the mind of the Light. Nor may it hinder the taking of a Thing of Power once it has been rightly claimed. Take your spell off the golden harp. You have no right to touch it with enchantment."

The mist swirled darker; the voice grew colder, more remote. "The harp is not spellbound, Old One. Take it from the sack."

Will bent down. He tried once more to pick up the sacking-wrapped harp, but it would not move; it might have been a rock rooted deep in the land. Then he pulled the sacking aside to uncover the harp, and took it up, and the shining gold thing came into his hand as lightly as ever it had.

He looked down at the sack. "There is something else there."

"Of course," said the Grey King.

Will ripped the half-rotted sacking so that it lay open; it still seemed quite empty, as it had from the first. Then he noticed in one fold a small highly-polished white stone, no bigger than a pebble. He bent to pick it up. It would not move.

He said slowly, "It is a warestone."

"Yes," the voice said.

"Your warestone. A channel for the Dark. So that when it is left in a certain place, you may know all that is happening in that place, and may put into it your will to make other things happen. It was hidden in that old sack all the time." A sudden memory flickered in his mind. "No wonder I lost my hold on the fox of the *milgwn*."

Out of the mist, laughter came. It was a terrifying sound, like the first rattle of an avalanche. Then

146

instead, and worse, the voice came whispering. "A warestone of the Dark has no value for the Light. Give it me."

"You had put it on Caradog Prichard's farm," Will said. "Why? He is your creature anyway, you have no need of a warestone for him."

"That fool is none of mine," the Grey King said contemptuously. "If the Dark showed itself to him he would melt with fear like butter in the sun. No, he is not of the Dark. But he is very useful. A man so wrapped in his own ill-will is a gift to the Dark from the earth. It is so easy to give him suitable ideas . . . Very useful, indeed."

Will said quietly. "There are such men, of an opposite kind, who unwittingly serve the Light too."

"Ah," said the voice slyly, "but not so many, Old One. Not so many, I think." It sharpened again, and the mist swirled colder. "Give me the warestone. It will not work against you, but neither will it work for you. It will always cleave to the earth at the touch of the Light — as would a warestone of yours, if you had one, at my touch."

"I have no need of one," Will said. "Certainly no need of yours. Take it."

"Stand away. I shall take it and be gone. And if in one night and one day you are not also gone, from this my land, you will cease to exist by the standards of men, Old One. You shall not hinder us, not with your six Signs nor your harp of gold." The voice rose and swelled suddenly like a high wind. "For our time is almost come, in spite of you, and the Dark is rising, *the Dark is rising!*"

The words roared through Will's mind as the mist swirled dark and chill round his face, obscuring everything, even the ground beneath his feet. He could no longer see the harp, but only feel it clutched close in both his arms. He staggered giddily, and a terrible chill struck into all the length of his body.

Then it was gone. And he stood in the lane between the hedges, with the harp clasped to his chest, and the valley was clear all about him under the grey sky, and at his feet an empty piece of old sacking lay.

Shakily Will bent and wrapped the harp again, and set off for Clwyd Farm.

He slipped upstairs to his room to hide the harp, calling a greeting to Aunt Jen. She called back over her shoulder without turning, stirring a pot carefully at the stove. But when Will came downstairs again, the big kitchen seemed full of people. His uncle and Rhys were roving restlessly about, faces taut with concern. John Rowlands had just come through the door.

"Did you see him?" Rhys burst out anxiously to Rowlands.

John Rowlands's weather-lined brown face gained a few extra lines as his eyebrows rose. "Who should I have seen?"

David Evans pulled out a chair and dropped wearily into it. He sighed. "Caradog Prichard was outside just now. There is no end to this madness. He claims that another of his sheep was worried by a dog this afternoon — killed, this one. He says that it happened right there in his yard, again, and that he and his wife saw everything. And he swears up and down that the dog was Pen."

"Waving his gun about, he was, the damn lunatic," Rhys said angrily. "He would have shot the dog for sure, if you and Pen had been here. Thank God you were not."

John Rowlands said mildly, "I am surprised he was not waiting for us at the gate."

"I told him you were out late on the mountain, after some ewes," said Will's uncle, his neat head bent, despondent. "No doubt the fool will be out there looking for you."

"Shoot a sheep he will, I shouldn't be surprised," John Rowlands said. "If he can find the black ewe, that is."

But David Evans was too shaken to smile. "Let him do that, and I will have him off to Tywyn police station, dogs or no dogs. I don't like it, John Rowlands. The man is acting as if . . . I don't know, I really think that his wits have begun to turn. Raving, he was. Dogs killing sheep is a bad thing, heaven knows, but he was acting as wild as if it was children had been killed. If he had had children. I think it is as well he has not."

"Pen has been with me all day, without a break," John Rowlands said, his deep voice tranquil.

"Of course he has," said Rhys. "But Caradog Prichard would not believe that even if he had watched you every minute of the day with his own eyes. He is that bad. And he will be back tomorrow, there is no doubt at all."

"Perhaps Betty Prichard will be able to make him see reason before then," Aunt Jen said. "Though she has never had much luck before, goodness knows. He must be a hard man to be married to, that one."

John Rowlands looked at Will's uncle. "What shall we do?"

"I don't know," David Evans said, shaking his head morosely. "What do you think?"

"Well," John Rowlands said, "I was thinking that if you are not using the Land-Rover in the morning, I might go very early up the valley and leave Pen for a few days with Idris Jones Ty-Bont."

Will's uncle lifted his head, his face brightening for the first time. "Good. Very good."

"Jones Ty-Bont owes you a favour, for borrowing the tractor this summer. He is a good fellow anyway. And one of his dogs is from the same litter as Pen."

"That is a very good idea," Rhys said simply. "And we are out of plugs for the chain saw. You can pick one up in Abergynolwyn coming back."

Rowlands laughed. "All settled, then."

"Mr Rowlands," Will said. "Could I come too?"

150

They had not noticed he was there; heads turned in surprise to where he stood on the stairs.

"Come and welcome," John Rowlands said.

"That would be nice," Aunt Jen said. "I was just thinking yesterday that we hadn't taken you to Tal y Llyn yet. That's the lake, up there. Idris Jones's farm is right next to it."

"Caradog Prichard will not dream that the dog might be there," said David Evans. "It will give him time to cool off."

"And if the sheep-killing goes on —" Rhys said. Deliberately he left the sentence hanging.

"There's a thought now," Will's aunt said. "We must make sure Caradog thinks Pen is still here. Then if he sees Pen with his own eyes savage a sheep again tomorrow, there will be a quick answer for him."

"Good, then," John Rowlands said. "Pen is at home having his supper, I think I will go and join him. We will leave at five-thirty, Will. Caradog Prichard is not the earliest riser in the world."

"Perhaps young Bran would like to go with you, being a Saturday," said David Evans, leaning back relaxed now in his chair.

"I don't think so," Will said.

The Pleasant Lake

Will expected to be the only one stirring in the house, at five in the morning, but his Aunt Jen was up before him. She gave him a cup of tea, and a big slab of homemade bread and butter.

"Cold out there, early," she said. "You'll do better with something inside you."

"Bread and butter tastes five times as good here as anywhere else," said Will. Glancing up as he chewed, he saw her watching him with a funny, wry half-smile.

"The picture of health you are," she said. "Just like your big brother Stephen, at your age. Nobody would guess how ill you were, not so long ago. But my goodness me, it's not exactly a rest cure we've been giving you. The fire, and all this business with the sheep-killing —"

"Exciting," said Will, muffled, through a mouthful.

"Well, yes," said Aunt Jen. "Indeed, in a place where nothing out of the ordinary ever happens, usually, from one year's end to the next. I think I have had enough excitement to be getting along with, for now."

Will said lightly, deliberately, "I suppose the last real stir was when Bran's mother came."

"Ah," his aunt said. Her pleasant, cosy face was unreadable. "You've heard about that, have you? I suppose John Rowlands told you. He is a kind soul, *Shoni mawr*, no doubt he had his reasons. Tell me, Will, have you had some sort of a quarrel with Bran?"

Will thought: *and that's what you wanted to ask me, with the cup of tea, because you are a kind soul too, and can feel Bran's distress ... And I wish I could be properly honest with you.*

"No," he said. "But losing Cafall has been so bad for him that I think he just wants to be alone. For a while."

"Poor lad." She shook her head. "Be patient with him. He's a lonely boy, and had a strange life, in some ways. It's been wonderful for him having you here, until this spoiled everything."

A small pain shot through Will's forearm; he clutched it, and found it came from the scar of the Light, his burned-in brand.

He said suddenly, "Did she never come back at all, ever, Auntie Jen? Bran's mother? How could she just go off and leave him, like that?"

"I don't know," his aunt said. "But no, there was no sign of her ever again."

"In one minute, to go away for ever ... I think that must bother Bran a lot."

She looked at him sharply. "Has he ever said anything about it?"

"Oh, no, of course not. We've never talked about that. I just felt — I'm just sure it must bother him, underneath."

"You're a funny boy yourself," said his aunt curiously. "Sometimes you sound like an old man. Comes from having so many brothers and sisters older than you, I suppose . . . Perhaps you understand Bran better than most boys could."

She hesitated for a moment, then drew her chair closer. "I will tell you something," she said, "in case it might help Bran. I know you have sense enough not to tell him about it. I think Gwen, his mother, had some great trouble in her past life that she could do nothing about, and that because of that she felt she had to give Bran a life that would be free of it. She knew Owen Davies was a good man and would look after the boy, but she also knew that she simply did not love Owen as deeply as he loved her, not enough to marry him. When things turn out like that, there is nothing a woman can do. It is kindest to go away." She paused. "Not kind to leave Bran, you might say."

"That was just exactly what I was going to say," said Will.

"Well," said his aunt. "Gwen said something to me, in those few days she was here, when we were alone once. I have never talked about it, but I have never forgotten. She said: *If you have once betrayed a great trust, you dare not let yourself be trusted*

154

again, because a second betrayal would be the end of the world. I don't know if you can understand that."

"You mean she was frightened of what she might do?"

"And more frightened of what she had done. Whatever it was."

"So she ran away. Poor Bran," said Will.

"Poor Owen Davies," said his aunt.

There was a gentle knock at the door, and John Rowlands put his head inside. "*Bore da*," he said. "Ready, Will?"

"*Bore da*, John," said Aunt Jen, smiling at him.

Pulling on his jacket, Will turned suddenly and gave her a clumsy hug. "Thank you, Aunt Jen."

The smile brightened with pleasure and surprise. "We'll see you when we see you," she said.

John Rowlands said, as he started the car outside the farm gate, "Fond of you, your auntie."

Will held open the door for Pen to scramble up; the dog jumped over the seat into the back, and lay docile on the floor.

"I'm fond of her too, very. So's my mum."

"Be careful then, won't you?' Rowlands said. His seamed brown face was innocent of all expression, but the words had force. Will looked at him rather coldly.

"What do you mean?"

"Well," Rowlands said carefully, turning the Land-Rover into the road. "I am not at all sure what it is that is going on all around us, Will *bach*, or where it is leading. But those men who know anything at all about the Light also know that there is a fierceness to its power, like the bare sword of the law, or the white burning of the sun." Suddenly his voice sounded to Will very strong, and very Welsh. "At the very heart, that is. Other things, like humanity, and mercy, and charity, that most good men hold more precious than all else, they do not come first for the Light. Oh, sometimes they are there; often, indeed. But in the very long run the concern of you people is with the absolute good, ahead of all else. You are like fanatics. Your masters, at any rate. Like the old Crusaders — oh, like certain groups in every belief, though this is not a matter of religion, of course. At the centre of the Light there is a cold white flame, just as at the centre of the Dark there is a great black pit bottomless as the Universe."

His warm, deep voice ended, and there was only the roar of the engine. Will looked out over the grey-misted fields, silent.

"There was a great long speech, now," John Rowlands said awkwardly. "But I was only saying, be careful not to forget that there are people in this valley who can be hurt, even in the pursuit of good ends."

Will heard again in his mind Bran's anguished cry as the dog Cafall was shot dead, and heard his cold dismissal: *go away, go away* ... And for a second another image, unexpected, flashed into his mind out of the past: the strong, bony face of Merriman his master, first of the Old Ones, cold in judgement of a much-loved figure who, through the frailty of being no more than a man, had once betrayed the cause of the Light.

He sighed. "I understand what you are saying," he said sadly. "But you misjudge us, because you are a man yourself. For us, there is only the destiny. Like a job to be done. We are here simply to save the world from the Dark. Make no mistake, John, the Dark *is* rising, and will take the world to itself very soon if nothing stands in its way. And if that should happen, then there would be no question ever, for anyone, either of warm charity or of cold absolute good, because nothing would exist in the world or in the hearts of men except that bottomless black pit. The charity and the mercy and the humanitarianism are for you, they are the only things by which men are able to exist together in peace. But in this hard case that we the Light are in, confronting the Dark, we can make no use of them. We are fighting a war. We are fighting for life or death — not for our life, remember, since we cannot die. For yours."

He reached his hand behind him, over the back of the seat, and Pen licked it with his floppy wet tongue.

"Sometimes," Will said slowly, "in this sort of a war, it is not possible to pause, to smoothe the way for one human being, because even that one small thing could mean an end of the world for all the rest."

A fine rain began to mist the windscreen. John Rowlands turned on the wipers, peering forward at the grey world as he drove. He said, "It is a cold world you live in, *bachgen*. I do not think so far ahead, myself. I would take the one human being over all the principle, all the time."

Will slumped down low in his seat, curling into a ball, pulling up his knees. "Oh, so would I," he said sadly. "So would I, if I could. It would feel a lot better inside me. But it wouldn't work."

Behind them, Pen leapt unexpectedly to his feet, barking. Will uncoiled like a startled snake; John Rowlands braked sharply, half-turning, and spoke swift and low to the dog in Welsh. But still Pen stood in the back of the Land-Rover stiff as a stuffed dog, barking furiously, and in the next moment, as if he were observing something outside himself, Will felt his own body jerk stiff as he felt the same force. His finger-nails drove into the palms of his hands.

John Rowlands did not stop the car, though he had slowed to a crawl. He gave one sharp look out of his near window at the moorland, through the mist, and accelerated again. In a moment or two Will felt the tension go out of his limbs, and sat back, gasping. The dog too stopped barking, and in the sudden loud silence lay down meekly on the floor as if he had never moved at all.

Rowlands said, with a tightness in his deep voice, "We have just come past the cottage. The empty cottage, where we lost the sheep."

Will said nothing. His breath was coming fast and shallow, as it had when he first came out of the worst of his illness, and he hunched his shoulders and bent his head beneath the fierce weight of the power of the Grey King.

John Rowlands drove faster, pulling the tough little car round blind slate-walled turns. The road curved across the valley; great new slopes rose on its eastern side, swooping up into the sky bare and grey, treacherous with scree. Everywhere they loomed over the gentle green fields, dominant, menacing. And then at last there were signs of side roads, and scattered grey slate-roofed houses, and before them, as Rowlands slowed for a crossroad, Will saw the lake Tal y Llyn.

His aunt had called it the loveliest lake in Wales, but lying dark there in the grey morning, it was more sinister than lovely. On its black still surface not a ripple stirred. It filled the valley floor. Above it reared the first slopes of Cader Idris, the mountain of the Grey King, and beyond, at the far end of the valley, a pass led through the hills — away, Will felt, towards the end of the world. He had himself under control now, but he could feel the tension quivering in his mind. The Grey King had felt his coming, and the awareness of his angry hostility was as clear as if it were shouted aloud. Will knew that it could not be long before one of the watchers, a peregrine curving high over the slopes, would catch clear sight of him. He did not know what would happen then.

John Rowlands turned the Land-Rover down a rough track, away from the lake, and before long they came to a farm tucked beneath the lowest slopes of Cader Idris. Will jumped out to open and close the gate, and as he trudged up into the farmyard he saw a small man in a flat cap come out of the house to greet the car. Dogs were barking. He could see one of them waiting a little way off where the farmer had left it: a sheepdog a little smaller than Pen, but with exactly the same black coat, and the splash of white under the chin.

Rowlands broke off an animated Welsh conversation as Will came up to them. "Idris, this is a new helper I have — David Evans's nephew Will, from England."

"How do you do, Mr Jones," Will said.

Idris Jones Ty-Bont twinkled at him as they shook hands; he had enormous and rather prominent dark eyes that made him look disconcertingly like a bush baby. "How are you, Will? I hear you have been having fun with our friend Caradog Prichard."

"We all have," John Rowlands said grimly. He gave a whistle over his shoulder, and Pen leapt out of the car, glanced up as if seeking permission to leave, and trotted off to greet the other black dog. They circled one another amiably, without barking.

"Lala there is his sister, believe it or not," Idris Jones said to Will. "Came from the same litter, they did, over Dinas way. That's a while ago, eh, John? Come along inside now, Megan has just made the tea."

160

In the warm kitchen, with stout, smiling Mrs
Jones who was almost twice the size of her neat
husband, the smell of frying bacon made Will rav-
enous all over again. He filled himself happily with
two fried eggs, thick slices of homecured bacon,
and hot flat Welshcakes, like miniature pancakes
flecked with currants. Mrs Jones began instantly
chattering away to John Rowlands in a contented
flow of Welsh, scarcely ever seeming to draw breath,
or to give way to a phrase or two in her husband's
light voice, or Rowlands's deep rumble. Clearly
she was enjoying relaying all the local gossip, and
collecting any that might emanate from Clwyd.
Will, full of bacon and well-being, had almost
stopped paying attention when he saw John Rowlands, listening, give a sudden start and sit forward,
taking his pipe out of his mouth.

Rowlands said, in English, "Up over the lake, did
you say, Idris?"

"That's right," Farmer Jones said, dutifully swit-
ching languages with a quick smile at Will. "Up on
a ledge. I didn't have a chance to get too close,
being in a hurry after my own sheep, but I am
almost sure it was a Pentref ewe. Not dead very
long, I think, the birds had not been at it enough
— maybe a day or two. What interested me was the
blood on the neck. Quite old, it was, very dark, must
have been on the fleece a lot longer than the sheep
had been dead. And for a sheep that must have been
already wounded, that slope was a hell of a funny
place to go. Well, I'll show you later."

161

Will and John Rowlands looked at one another.

"You think it's *that* sheep?" Will said. "The one that vanished?"

"I think it may be," John Rowlands said.

But later, when Idris Jones took them to see the ewe, he would not let Will come close enough to see.

"Not a nice sight, *bachgen*," he said, looking doubtfully at Will and resettling the cap on his head. "A sheep when the ravens have been at her for a day or two is a bit of a mess, if you're not accustomed to it . . . wait you here a minute or two, we will be straight back."

"All right," Will said, resigned. But as the two men went on up the steep, slippery mountainside, he sat hastily down in a sudden fit of giddiness, and knew that it certainly would not have been a good idea for him to have gone further on. They were on a slope rising above the lake, a broad unprotected sweep of scree and poor grass broken by ledges and outcrops of granite. Further down the valley the mountain was clothed in dark forests of spruce trees, but here the land was bare, inhospitable. The dead sheep lay on a ledge that seemed to Will totally inaccessible; high above his head it jutted out of the mountain, and the pathetic white heap lying on it was not visible from where he sat now. Nor could he see John Rowlands and Idris Jones, climbing higher with the two black dogs.

Two hundred feet below lay the lake, its stillness broken only by one small dinghy moving lazily out from the small anglers' hotel that nestled beneath the mountains at the opposite side. Will could see no other sign of life anywhere on the rest of the lake, or on either side of the valley. The land seemed gentler now, with subtle colour everywhere, for the sun was breaking out fitfully between scudding clouds.

Then there was a scuffling and stumbling above him, and John Rowlands came down the steep slope, planting his heels firmly into the shale lying loose in the thin grass. Idris Jones and the dogs followed. Rowlands's lined face was bleak.

He said, "That is the same ewe all right, Will. But how she could have got out of that cottage and up here is just beyond me. It makes no sense at all." He glanced over his shoulder at Idris Jones, who was shaking his birdlike head in distress. "Nor to Idris either. I have been telling him the story."

"Oh," Will said sadly, without bothering now to dissemble, "it was not very complicated really. The *milgwn* took her."

He saw from the corner of his eye that Idris Jones Ty-Bont stood suddenly very still, up on the slope, staring at him. Avoiding the farmer's eye, he sat there hugging his knees against his chest, and looked up at John Rowlands unguardedly for the first time, with the eyes not of a boy but of an Old One. Time was growing short, and he was tired of pretence.

"The king of the *milgwn*," he said. "The chief of the foxes of the Brenin Llwyd. He is the biggest

163

of all of them, and the most powerful, and his master has given him the way of doing many things. He is no more than a creature, still, but he is not at all . . . ordinary. For instance, he is now at this moment just exactly the colour of Pen, so that it would be hard for any man who, with his own eyes, saw him attacking a sheep, not to think for certain that it was Pen he was seeing attack the sheep."

John Rowlands was gazing at him, his dark eyes bright as polished stone. He said slowly, "And maybe before that he might have been just exactly the colour of Cafall, so that also anyone else might have thought —"

"Yes," Will said. "They might."

Rowlands shook his head abruptly as if to cast a weight from it. "I think it is time we went down off this mountain, Idris boy," he said firmly, heaving Will to his feet.

"Yes," said Idris Jones hastily. "Yes, yes." He followed them, looking totally bemused, as if he had just heard a sheep bark like a dog and were trying to find a way of believing what he had heard.

The dogs trotted ahead of them, turning protectively now and then to make sure they followed. John Rowlands very soon released Will to walk alone, for single file was the only possible way down the winding, steep path, made by sheep and seldom used by men. Will was halfway down to the lake before he fell.

He could never explain, afterwards, how he came to stumble. He could only have said, very simply, that the mountain shrugged — and even John Rowlands in the height of trustfulness could not have been expected to believe that. Nevertheless, the mountain did shrug, through the malice of its master the Brenin Llwyd, so that a piece of the path beneath Will's feet jumped perceptibly to one side and back again, like a cat humping its back, and Will saw it with sick horror only in the moment that he lost his balance and went rolling down. He heard the men shout and was aware of a flurry of movement as Rowlands dived to grab him. But he was already rolling, tumbling, and it was only a ledge of granite, jutting as the ledge on which they had found the dead sheep, that caught him from rolling the full hundred-foot drop down to the edge of the lake. He came a great thud against the jagged shelf of rock, and cried out in pain as a shaft of fire seemed to shoot blazing up his left arm. But the rock had saved him. He lay still.

Gentle as a mother, John Rowlands felt along the bone of his arm. His face was a strange colour, where the blood had drained away beneath the tan. "*Duw*," he said huskily, "you are a lucky one, Will Stanton. That is going to hurt a good deal for the next few days, but it is not broken anywhere so far as I can tell. And it might well have been in smithereens."

"And the boy at the bottom of Llyn Mwyngil!" Idris Jones said shakily, straightening up and trying to recover his lost breath. "How the devil did you manage to fall like that, *bachgen*? We were not going

so very fast at all, but such a speed you went
down —" He whistled softly, and took off his cap
to wipe his brow.

"Gently does it," said John Rowlands, putting
Will carefully back on his feet. "Are you all right
to walk, now? Not hurt anywhere else?"

"I shall be okay. Honestly. Thank you." Will was
trying to look around at Idris Jones. "Mr Jones?
What was that you called the lake?"

Jones looked at him blankly. "What?"

"You said, the boy might have been at the bottom
of the lake. Didn't you? But you didn't say Tal y
Llyn, you called it by some other name. Llyn
something else."

"Llyn Mwyngil. That is its proper name, the old
Welsh name." Jones was looking at him in a kind
of dazed wonder, clearly suspecting the fall had
knocked Will on the head. He added absently, "It
is a nice name but not much used these days, even
on the Ordnance Survey . . . like Bala too. Now that
should be Llyn Tegid as it always was, but they do
no more now anywhere than call it Bala Lake . . ."

Will said, "Llyn Mwyngil, what does it mean in
English?"

"Well . . . the lake in the pleasant place. Pleasant
retreat. Whatever."

"The pleasant lake," Will said. "No wonder I
fell. The pleasant lake."

"Yes, you could put it that way, loosely, I suppose." Idris Jones collected his wits suddenly and
turned in baffled anguish. "John Rowlands, what is

the matter with this mad boy you have found, standing up here talking semantics on a mountain, when he has just come close to breaking his neck? Get him down to the farm before he falls down in a fit and starts speaking with tongues."

John Rowlands's deep chuckle had relief in it. "Come on, Will."

Plump Mrs Jones clucked over Will in concern and put a cold compress on his forearm. Nobody would hear of his doing anything, or going anywhere. The patchy sunshine was warmer now, and Will found it not unpleasant at all to lie on his back in the grass near the farmhouse, with Pen's cold nose pushing at his ear, and watch the clouds scud across the pale blue sky. John Rowlands decided that he would go to Abergynolwyn, near by, to fetch the spark plug Rhys wanted from the garage there. Idris Jones discovered errands that meant he should go too. They both announced firmly that Will should stay with Mrs Jones and the dogs, and rest. He felt that they were still recovering from his fall themselves, treating him as a fragile piece of china which, since it had magically survived without breakage, should be set very carefully on a shelf and not moved for a special conciliatory length of time.

The Land-Rover chugged away with the two men. Mrs Jones fussed amiably to and fro until she had satisfied herself that Will was not in pain, or any distress, and then went off and settled to pastry-making in her kitchen.

For a while Will sat playing idly with the dogs, thinking of the Grey King in a mixture of brief triumph, resentment, belligerence, and nervousness of what might be going to happen next. For there was no escape now. He had known it, somehow, even when they had left that morning. His way lay firmly on into the middle of the heartland of the Brenin Llwyd. *By the pleasant lake the Sleepers lie ... On Cadfan's Way where the kestrels call ...* It had never occurred to him to follow the simplest route out of the conundrum, and go out and walk along Cadfan's Way until it led him to a lake. But there would have been no difference in the end. Sooner or later he would have come here, to Tal y Llyn, Llyn Mwyngil, the lake in the pleasant place under the shadow of the Grey King.

Taking Pen with him, and leaving a patient resigned Lala behind, he strolled beyond the farm gate and out down the slate-fenced lane. A few late blackberries hung down over the grassy bank, and a woodlark sang behind the fence; it might almost have been summer. But though the sun shone, in the distance over the brambles Will could see mist round Cader Idris's peaks.

He was in a dreamy, suspended state of mind, due partly to the aspirin Mrs Jones had made him take for the pain in his arm, when all at once he saw a boy come hurtling down the lane towards him on a bicycle. Will jumped to one side. There was a squealing of brakes, a flurry of kicked-up slate dust, and the boy collapsed in a pile of legs and spinning wheels on the other side of the lane. His cap tumbled off and Will saw the white hair. It was Bran.

His face was damp with sweat; his shirt clung stickily to his chest, and his breath came in great gulps. He had no time for greeting, or explanation.

"Will — Pen — get him away from here, hide him! Caradog Prichard found out. He's coming. He is as mad as a hatter, he swears he's going to kill Pen whatever, and he's on his way here now, with his gun . . ."

The Warestone

Bran got to his feet, brushing off dust and grass.

Will gaped at him. "You've just cycled all the way from Clwyd?"

Bran nodded. "Caradog Prichard came roaring up in his van this morning, looking for Pen. He is dead set on shooting him. I was frightened, Will. The way he looks, he is not like a man at all. And I think he had been hunting all night for John Rowlands and Pen, he was all creased looking, and not shaved." His breath was coming more normally now. He picked up his bicycle. "Come on. Quick!"

"Where shall we go?"

"I don't know. Anywhere. Just away from here." He tugged his bicycle up over the bank edging the lane at the left, and led them off through bushes and trees towards the open moorland that stretched back down the valley, away from the lake.

Will scrambled after him, with Pen at his side. "But does he really know we're here? He couldn't."

"That's the only part I don't understand," Bran said. "He was having a big argument with your

cousin Rhys, about where Pen was, and then suddenly he stopped in the middle of it and went very
quiet. It was almost as if he were listening. Then
he said, *I know where they are gone. They are gone
to the lake.* Just like that. Rhys tried to talk him out
of it, but I don't think that worked. Somehow
Prichard just knew. I'm positive he's on his way to
Ty-Bont. Pen! Hey!" He whistled, and the dog
paused ahead, waiting for them. They were walking
on rising ground now, through waist-high bracken,
on a meandering sheep path.

"How did you get here before him, then?" Will
said.

Bran looked over his shoulder with a quick grin;
he had moved ahead on the path, pushing his bike.
Something seemed to have transformed him out of
the figure of despair Will had seen the day before.

"Caradog Prichard will not be too pleased about
that," Bran said solemnly. "I had my clasp knife in
my pocket, you see, and I happened to be passing
his van when he was not looking, and I stuck it in
his back tyre, and gave it a good jerk. And while I
was at it I stuck it in his spare tyre too. You know
the way he has the spare bolted onto the side of the
van? A mistake, that is, he should keep it inside."

The tension inside Will snapped like a breaking
spring, and he began to laugh. Once he had started,
it was hard to stop. Bran paused, grinning, and then
the grin became a chuckle and before long they
were reeling with laughter, roaring, tottering, clut-

ching at one another, in a wild fit of chortling mirth with the dog Pen leaping about them happily.

"Imagine his face," Will gasped, "when he goes tearing off in the van and poof! the tyre goes flat, and he gets out furious and changes it, and goes tearing off again, and poof —"

They collapsed again, gurgling.

Bran took off his dark glasses and wiped them. "Mind you," he said, "it is going to make everything worse in the long run, because he will know very well somebody cut the tyres on purpose, and that will just make him wilder than ever."

"Worth it," Will said. Controlled again, but cheerful, he gave Bran a sideways, rather shy glance. "Hey," he said. "It was nice of you to come, considering."

"Oh, well," Bran said. He put the glasses back on, retreating once more into inscrutability; his white hair lay in damp-darkened lines across his forehead. He seemed about to say something else, but changed his mind. "Come on!" he said; jumped on his bicycle and began pedalling erratically off along the weaving path through the bracken.

Will began to run. "Where are we going?"

"Goodness knows!"

They careered along in a happy, lunatic chase through the valley: over open slopes, down into hollows; up over ridges, in and out of rounded, lichened rocks; through grass and bracken and heather and gorse, and quite often, on damper ground near one of the little streams that fed the

172

river, through reeds and iris leaves. They had come a long way from the lake; this was the main valley land now, open grazing land, merging into the arable fields of Clwyd and Prichard's Farm further down, past the jutting hills.

Suddenly Bran skidded, tumbling sideways. Thinking he had fallen, Will went to help, but Bran grabbed his arm and pointed urgently across the moorland. "Over there! On the road! There's a curve a long way down where you can see cars coming, before they get here — I'm almost sure I just saw Prichard's van!"

Will grabbed Pen by the collar and looked wildly about. "We must get under cover — behind those rocks over there?"

"Wait! I see where we are! There's a better place, just up here — come on!" Bran bumped off again. The big sheepdog slipped from Will's hand and bounded after him. Will ran. They rounded a group of near-by trees, and there beyond it was the glimmer of grey stone and slate, behind a low ruined wall. The cottage looked quite different from behind. Will did not recognize it until too late. Bran had shot inside, thumping open the broken back door, before he could call to prevent him, and then there was no alternative but to follow.

Naked to the eye of the Grey King, feeling the force of the Dark pressing sudden and strong on him like a huge hand, he stumbled after the dog and the white-haired boy into the cottage from which the *milgwn* had stolen the wounded sheep, the cottage where Owen Davies had fought Caradog Prichard for the woman who had borne and deserted Bran; the cottage haunted, now more than ever, by the malice of the rising Dark.

But Bran, propping his bicycle against a wall, was bright and unaffected. "Isn't this perfect? It's an old shepherd's hut, no one's used it for years . . . quick, over here — keep your head down —"

They crouched beside the window, Pen lying quiet beside them, and saw through the jagged-edged hole the small grey van passing perhaps fifty yards away on the road. Prichard was driving slowly. They could see him peering from side to side, scouring the land. He glanced incuriously at the cottage, and drove on.

The van disappeared along the road to Tal y Llyn. Bran leaned back against the wall. "Whew! Lucky!"

But Will was paying no attention. He was too much occupied with shielding his mind from the raging malevolence of the Grey King. He said through his teeth, the words coming slow and dragging, "Let's . . . get . . . away . . . from . . . here . . ."

Bran stared at him, but asked no questions. "All right, then. *Tyrd yma*, Pen." He turned to the dog, and suddenly his voice came high as the wind in the telegraph wires. "Pen! What is it? Look at him, Will!"

The dog lay flat on his stomach, his four legs splayed outwards, his head down sideways against the floor. It was horrible, unnatural; a position impossible for any normal living creature. A faint whistling whine came from his throat, but he did not move. It was as if invisible pins held him forced flat against the ground.

"Pen!" Will said in horror. "Pen!" But he could not lift the dog's head. The animal was not paralysed by any natural circumstance. Only enchantment could force him so hard into the earth that no living hand could move him.

"What is it?" There was fear in Bran's face.

"It is the Brenin Llwyd," Will said. His tone seemed to Bran deeper than before, more resonant. "It is the Brenin Llwyd, and he has forgotten the bargain that he made when we spoke yesterday. He has forgotten that he gave me one night and one day."

"*You spoke to him?*" Bran heard his voice come out in a broken whisper, and he crouched there motionless beside the window. But again Will was paying no attention. He spoke half to himself, in this same strange adult voice. "It is sent not at me but at the dog. It is indirect, then, a device. I wonder . . ."

He broke off and glanced at Bran, waving a finger at him in warning. "You may watch me if you will, though it would be better not, but you must say nothing, and make no move. Not one."

"All right," Bran said.

He watched, crouching on the dirty, broken slate floor in one corner, and he saw Will move to the middle of the room, to stand beside the hideously prostrate dog.

Will bent and picked up a broken piece of wood, from the litter of the empty years that lay scattered everywhere. He touched it to the ground before his feet and, turning, drew a circle about Pen and himself on the floor with the tip of the stick. Where the circle was drawn, a ring of blue flame sprang up, and when it was complete, Will relaxed and stood full upright, like someone freed of a great burden that had been weighing him down. He raised the stick vertically in the air over his head, so that it touched the low ceiling, and he said some words in a language that Bran did not understand.

The cottage seemed to grow very dark, so that Bran's weak eyes, blinking, could see nothing but the blue ring of cold fire and Will's form shadowy in the middle of it. But then he saw that another light was beginning to glow in the room: a small blue spark, somewhere in the far corner, steadily growing brighter until it blazed with such intensity that he was forced to look away.

Will said something, sharp and angry, in the language that Bran could not understand. The circle of blue flames flared high and then low, high and low, high and low, three times, and then suddenly went out. Instantly the cottage was full of daylight again, and the brilliant star of light nowhere to be seen. Bran let out a long slow breath, staring about the room to try and see where the light had been. But the room seemed now so different and ordinary that he could not tell. Nor could he imagine where the circle had been drawn, though he knew it had been round Will.

Will, standing there unmoving, was the only thing in the room that seemed not to have changed utterly, in that one second — and even he seemed now once more different, a boy as he had been, but glaring round the floor irritably as if peering for an errant marble that had rolled away.

He glanced at Bran and said crossly, "Come and look at this." Then without waiting, while Bran scrambled nervously up, he crossed to the far corner of the room, crouched, and began riffling through a small pile of bits of stone that lay there, random-scattered and dusty, among the debris. Pushing them aside, he cleared a space in which one small white pebble lay alone. He said to Bran, "Pick it up."

Puzzled, Bran reached out and took the pebble. But he found that he could not pick it up. He worked at it with his fingers. He stood up, straddled it, and tried with thumbs and forefingers to pull it up from the floor. He stared at the pebble, and then at Will.

"It's part of the floor. It must be."

"The floor's made of slate," Will said. He still sounded cross, almost petulant.

"Well ... yes. No stones in slate, true. But all the same it's fixed, somehow. Bit of quartz. It won't budge."

"It is a warestone," Will said, his voice flat now, and weary. "The awareness of the Grey King. I might have guessed. It is, in this place, his eyes and his ears and his mouth. Through it — just through the fact of its lying there — he not only knows everything that happens in this place, but can send out his power to do certain things. Only certain things. Not any very great magic. But, for instance, he is able so to paralyse Pen there that we can no more move him than we can move the warestone itself."

Bran knelt in distress beside the dog, and stroked the head flattened so unnaturally against the floor. "But if Caradog Prichard tracks us here — he might, his dogs might — then he will just shoot Pen where he lies. And there will be nothing we can do to help."

Will said bitterly, "That's the idea."

"But Will, that can't happen. You've got to do something!"

"There is just one thing that I can do," Will said. "Though obviously I can't tell you what it is, with that thing there. It means I shall have to borrow your bicycle. But I'm not too sure whether you should stay here alone."

"Somebody's got to. We can't leave Pen like that. Not on his own."

"I know. But the warestone . . ." Will glared at the pebble as if it were some infuriating small child sitting there clutching an object too precious for it to hold. "It's not a particularly powerful weapon,"

178

he said, "but it's one of the oldest. We all use them, both the Light and the Dark. There are rules, sort of. None of us can actually be affected by a warestone — only observed. That wretched pebble can give the Grey King an idea of what I do and say here. A general idea, like an image — it's not as specific as a television set, mercifully. It can't do anything to harm me, or stop me doing what I want to do — except through the control it has over objects. I mean, it can't actually affect me, because I am an Old One, but it *can* transmit the power of the Dark — or of the Light, if it happened to belong to an Old One — to affect men, and animals, and things of the earth. It can stop Pen from moving, and therefore stop me from moving him. You see? So that if you stay here, there's no knowing what exactly it's able to do to you."

Bran said obstinately: "I don't care." He sat cross-legged by the dog. "It can't kill me, can it?"

"Oh, no."

"Well, then. I'm staying. Go on, off with the bike."

Will nodded, as if that was what he had been expecting. "I'll be as quick as I can. But take care. Stay very wide awake. If anything does happen, it will come in the way you least expect."

Then he was gone out of the door, and Bran was left in the cottage with a dog pressed impossibly flat against the slate floor by an invisible high wind, staring at a small white stone.

"Good day, Mrs Jones. How are you?"

"Well, thank you, Mr Prichard. And you?"

Caradog Prichard's plump pale face was glistening with sweat. Impatience swept away his Welsh politeness. He said abruptly, "Where is John Rowlands?"

"John?' said cosy Megan Jones, wiping floury hands on her apron. "There now, what a shame, you have missed him. Idris and he went off to Abergynolwyn half an hour ago. They will not be back until dinner, and that will be late today . . . You want to see him urgently, is it, Mr Prichard?"

Caradog Prichard stared at her vacantly and did not answer. He said, in a high tight voice, "Is Rowlands's dog here?"

"Pen? Goodness no," Mrs Jones said truthfully. "Not with John gone." She smiled amiably at him. "Is it the man you want to see, or the dog, then? Well, indeed, you are welcome to wait for them here, though as I say, it may be quite a time. Let me get you a cup of tea, Mr Prichard, and a nice fresh Welshcake."

"No," said Prichard, running his hand distractedly through his raw red hair. "No . . . no, thank you." He was so lost in his own mind that he scarcely seemed to be aware of her at all. "I will be off to town and see if I find them there. At the Crown, perhaps . . . John Rowlands has some business with Idris Ty-Bont, does he?'

"Oh," said Mrs Jones comfortably, "he is just visiting. Since he had something to do in Abergy-

nolwyn anyway. Just a call, you know, Mr Prichard.
Like your own." She beamed innocently at him.

"Well," said Caradog Prichard. "Thank you very
much. Good-bye."

Megan Jones looked after him as he swung the
grey van hastily round and drove away down the
lane. Her smile faded. "Not a nice man," she said
to the farmyard at large. "And something is going
on behind those little eyes of his that is not nice *at
all*. A very lucky thing it was that young Will
happened to take that dog for a walk just now."

Will pedalled hard, blessing the valley road for its
winding flatness, and freewheeling only when his
pounding heart seemed about to leap right out of
his chest. He rode one handed. He had said nothing
about his hurt arm, and Bran had not noticed, but
it hurt abominably if he so much as touched the
handlebars with his left hand. He tried not to think
about the way it would feel when carrying the
golden harp.

That was the only thing to be done, now. The
music of the harp was the only magic within his
reach that would release Pen from the power of the
warestone. In any case, it was time now to bring the
harp to the pleasant lake, to accomplish its deeper
purpose. Everything was coming together, as if two
roads led to the same mountain pass; he could only
hope that the pass would not be blocked by some
obstacle able to hinder both at once. This time more
than ever, the matter of holding the Dark at bay

depended as much on the decisions and emotions of men as on the strength of the Light. Perhaps even more.

Broken sunlight flickered in and out of his eyes, as clouds scudded briskly over the sky. At least, he thought wryly, we've got a good day for it all. His wheels sang on the road; he was nearly at Clwyd Farm now. He wondered how he was to explain his sudden arrival, and equally sudden departure afterwards, to Aunt Jen. She would probably be the only one there. She must have been there for Caradog Prichard's appearance earlier that morning, and the changing of his two mutilated tyres. Perhaps he could say that he had come to get something to help put Prichard off the scent, to keep him from finding Pen ... something John Rowlands had suggested ... but still he would have to leave the house with the golden harp. Aunt Jen would not be likely to let that sacking-swathed object past her sharp eye without at least inquiring what was wrapped up in there. And what possible reason could anyone have, least of all her nephew, for not letting her see?

Will wished, not for the first time, that Merriman were with him, to ease such difficulties. For a Master of the Light, it was no great matter to transport beings and objects not only through space but through time, in the twinkling of an eye. But for the youngest of the Old Ones, however acute his need, that was a talent too large.

He came to the farm; rode in; pushed through the back door. But when he called, no one came. He realized suddenly with a great lightening of the spirits that he had seen no cars in the yard outside. Both his aunt and uncle must have gone out; that was one piece of luck, at any rate. He ran upstairs to his bedroom, said the necessary words to release the golden harp from protection, and ran down again with it under his arm, a rough sacking-wrapped bundle of odd triangular shape. He was halfway across the yard to the bicycle when a Land-Rover chugged in through the gate.

For a second Will froze in panic; then he walked slowly, carefully, to the bicycle, and turned it ready to leave.

Owen Davies climbed out of the car and stood looking at him. He said, "Was it you left the gate open?"

"Oh, gosh." Will was genuinely shocked: he had committed the classical farm sin, without even noticing. "Yes, I did, Mr Davies. That's awful. I'm most terribly sorry."

Owen Davies, thin and earnest, shook his flat-capped head in reproof. "One of the most important things to remember, it is, to shut any gate you have opened on a farm. You do not know what livestock of your uncle's might have slipped out, that should have been kept in. I know you are English, and no doubt a city boy, but that is no excuse."

"I know," Will said. "And I'm not even a city boy. I really am sorry. I'll tell Uncle David so."

Taken aback by this implication of honest confidence, Owen Davies surfaced abruptly from the pool of righteousness that had threatened to swallow him. "Well," he said. "Let us forget it this time, both of us. I dare say you will not do it again."

His gaze drifted sideways a little. "Is that Bran's bike you have there? Did he come with you?"

Will pressed the shrouded harp tight between his elbow and his side. "I borrowed it. He was out riding, and I was . . . up the valley, walking, and I saw him, and we thought we'd have a go at flying a big model plane I've been making." He patted the bundle under his arm, swinging his leg over the bicycle saddle at the same time. "So I'm going back now. Is that all right? You don't need him for anything?"

"Oh, no," Owen Davies said. "Nothing at all."

"John Rowlands took Pen to Mr Jones at Ty-Bont all safe and sound," Will said brightly. "I'm supposed to be having dinner there, late-ish Mrs Jones said — would it be all right if I took Bran back with me too, Mr Davies? Please?"

The usual expression of alarmed propriety came over Owen Davies's thin face. "Oh, no, now, Mrs Jones is not expecting him, there is no need to bother her with another —"

Unexpectedly, he broke off. It was as if he heard something, without understanding it. Puzzled, Will saw his face become oddly bemused, with the look of a man dreaming a dream that he has dreamed often but never been able to translate. It was a look he would never have expected to find on the face of a man so predictable and uncomplicated as Bran's father.

Owen Davies stared him full in the face, which was even more unusual. He said, "Where did you say you and Bran were playing?"

Will's dignity ignored the last word. He kicked at the bicycle pedal. "Out on the moor. Quite a long way up the valley, near the road. I don't know how to describe it exactly — but more than halfway to Mr Jones's farm."

"Ah," Owen Davies said vaguely. He blinked at Will, apparently back in his usual nervous person. "Well, I daresay it would be all right if Bran goes to dinner as well. John Rowlands being there — goodness knows Megan Jones is used to feeding a lot of mouths. But you must be sure to tell him he must be home before dark."

"Thank you!" said Will, and made off before he could change his mind, carefully closing the gate after he had ridden through. He shouted a farewell, with just time to notice Bran's father's hand slowly raised as he rode away.

But he was not many yards along the road, riding awkwardly one-handed and slowly with the harp clutched in his aching left arm, before all thought of Owen Davies was driven from his head by the Grey King. Now the valley was throbbing with power and malevolence. The sun was at its highest point, though no more than halfway up the sky in that November day. The last part of the time for the fulfilling of Will's only separate quest had begun. His mind was so much occupied with the unspoken beginnings of battle that it was all his body could do to push the bicycle, and himself, slowly along the road.

He paid little attention when a Land-Rover swished past him, going fast in the same direction. Several cars had passed him already, on both journeys, and in this part of the country Land-Rovers were common. There was no reason at all why this one should have differed from the rest.

The Cottage on the Moor

Alone with the motionless sheepdog, Bran went again to the pile of rubble in the corner of the room and stared at the warestone. So small, so ordinary: it was just like any other of the white quartz pebbles scattered over the land. He bent again and tried to pick it up, and felt the same throb of disbelief when it would not move. It was like the dreadful splayed attitude in which Pen lay. He was looking at the impossible.

It occurred to him to wonder why he was not afraid. Perhaps it was because part of his mind did still believe these things impossible, even while he saw them clearly. What could a pebble do to him? He went to the door of the cottage and stood staring across the valley, towards Bird Rock. The Craig was hard to see from here: an insignificant dark hump, dwarfed by the mountain ridge behind. Yet that too had held the impossible; he had gone down into the depths of that rock, and in an enchanted cavern

encountered three Lords of the High Magic there
... Bran had a sudden image of the bearded figure
in the sea-blue cloak, of the eyes from the hooded
face holding his own, and felt a strange urgent
warmth in the remembering. He would never forget
that figure, clearly the greatest of the three. There
was something particular and close about him. He
had even known Cafall.

Cafall.

*"Never fear, boy. The High Magic would never
take your dog from you ... Only the creatures of the
earth take away from one another, boy. All creatures,
but man more than any. Life they take ... Beware
your own race, Bran Davies — they are the only ones
who will ever hurt you ..."*

The pain of loss that Bran had begun to learn to
conceal struck into him like an arrow. In a great
rush his mind filled with pictures of Cafall as a
wobble-legged puppy, Cafall following him to
school, Cafall learning the signals and commands
of the working sheepdog, Cafall wet with rain, the
long hair pressed flat in a straight parting along his
spine, Cafall running, Cafall drinking from a stream,
Cafall asleep with his chin warm on Bran's foot.

Cafall dead.

He thought of Will then. It was Will's fault. If
Will had never brought him to —

"No," Bran said aloud suddenly. He turned and
glared at the warestone. Was it trying to turn his
mind to thinking ill of Will, and so to divide them?
Will had said, after all, that the Dark might try to

reach at him in some way he would least expect. That was it, for sure. He was being influenced subtly to turn against Will. Bran felt pleased with himself for noticing so soon.

"You can save the effort," he said jeeringly to the warestone. "It won't work, see?"

He went back to the doorway and looked out at the hills. His mind drifted back to thought of Cafall. It was hard to keep away from the last image: the worst, yet precious because it was the closest. He heard again the shot, and the way it had echoed round the yard. He heard his father saying, as Cafall lay bleeding his life out and Caradog Prichard sneered with success: *Cafall was going for the sheep, there is no question . . . I cannot say that I would not have shot him myself in Caradog's place. That is the right of it . . .*

The right, the right. So very sure his father was always, of the right and the wrong. His father and all his father's friends in chapel, and most of all the minister with his certain-sure preaching of good and bad, and the right way to live. For Bran it was a pattern of discipline: chapel twice on Sundays, listen and sit still without fidgeting, and do not commit the sins the Good Book forbids. For his father it was more: prayer meetings, sometimes twice a week, and always the necessity of behaving the way people expected a deacon to behave. There was nothing wrong with chapel and all of that, but Bran knew his father gave it more of himself than any other chapel member he had ever met. He was like a driven man, with his anxious face and hunched shoulders, weighed down by a sense of guilt that Bran had never been able to fathom for himself. There was no lightness in their lives; his father's endless meaningless penance would not allow it. Bran had never been allowed to go to the cinema in Tywyn, and on Sundays he could do nothing at all except go to chapel and walk the hills. His father was reluctant to let him go to school concerts and plays. It had even taken John Rowlands a long time to persuade him to let Bran play the harp in contests at *eisteddfodau*. It was as if Owen Davies kept both of them, himself and Bran, locked up in a little box in the valley, bleak and lonely, out of contact with all the bright things of life; as if they were condemned to a life in jail.

Bran thought: *It's not fair. All I had was Cafall, and now even Cafall is gone* . . . He could feel grief swelling in his throat, but he swallowed hard and gritted his teeth, determined not to cry. Instead rage and resentment grew in his mind. What right had his father to make everything so grim? They were no different from other people . . .

But that's wrong, said a voice in his mind. You are different. You are the freak with the white hair, and the pale skin that will not brown in the sun, and the eyes that cannot stand bright light. Whitey, they call you at school, and Paleface, and there is one boy from up the valley who makes the old sign against the Evil Eye in your direction if he thinks you are not looking. They don't like you. Oh, you're different, all right. Your father and your face have made you feel different all your life, you would be a freak inside even if you tried to dye your hair, or paint your skin.

Bran strode up and down the cottage room, furious and yet puzzled. He banged one hand against the door. He felt as though his head were about to burst. He had forgotten the warestone. It did not occur to him that this haunting too might be brought by the subtle workings of the Dark. Everything seemed to have vanished from the world except the resentful fury against his father that flooded his mind.

And then outside the cottage's broken front door there was the crunch and squeal of a car drawing up, and Bran looked out just in time to see his father jump out of the Land-Rover and stride towards the cottage.

He stood still, his head singing with rage and surprise. Owen Davies pushed open the door and stood looking at him.

"I thought you would be here," he said. Bran said curtly. "Why?"

His father made the strange ducking movement of his head that was one of his familiar nervous gestures. "Will was up at the farm, fetching something, and he said you were both up here, somewhere . . . he should be along soon."

Bran was standing stiffly. "Why are you here? Did Will make you think something was wrong?"

"Oh, no, no," Owen Davies said hastily. "Well then, what —"

But his father had seen Pen. He stood very still for a moment. Then he said gently, "But something is wrong, isn't it?"

Bran opened his mouth, and shut it again.

Owen Davies came further into the room and bent over the helpless sheepdog. "How is he hurt, then? Was it a fall? I never saw an animal lie so . . ." He stroked the dog's head, and felt along his legs, then moved his hand to pick up one paw. Pen gave an almost inaudible whine, and rolled his eyes. The paw would not move. It was not rigid, or stiff; it was simply bound fast to the earth, like the warestone. Bran's father tried each of the four paws in turn, and each time could not move any a fraction of an inch. He stood up and backed slowly away, staring at Pen. Then he raised his head to look at Bran, and in his eyes a terrible fear was mingled with accusation.

"*What have you been doing, boy?*"

Bran said, "It is the power of the Brenin Llwyd."

"Nonsense!" Owen Davies said sharply. "Superstitious nonsense! I will *not* have you talk of those old pagan stories as if they were true."

"All right, Da," Bran said. "Then it is superstitious nonsense that you cannot move the dog."

"It is some kind of rigor of the joints," his father said, looking at Pen. "It seems to me he has broken his back, and the nerves and the muscles are all

192

stiffened up." But there was no conviction in his voice.

"There is nothing wrong with him. He is not hurt. He is like that because —" Bran felt suddenly that it would be going much too far to tell his father about the warestone. He said instead, "It is the malice of the Brenin Llwyd. Through his trickery Cafall was shot when he should not have been, and now he is trying to make it easy for that crazy Caradog Prichard to get Pen as well!"

"Bran, Bran!" His father's voice was high with agitation. "You must not let yourself be carried away so by Cafall dying. There was no help for it, *bachgen*, he turned into a sheep-chaser and there was no help for it. A killer dog has to be killed."

Bran said, trying to keep his voice from trembling, "He was not a killer dog, Da, and you do not know what you are talking about. Because if you do, why can you not get Pen to move one centimetre from where he is lying? It is the Brenin Llwyd, I tell you, and there is nothing you can do."

And he could tell from the apprehension in Owen Davies's eyes that deep down, he believed it was the truth.

"I should have known," his father said miserably. "When I found you here in this place, I should have known such things were happening."

Bran stared at him. "What do you mean?"

His father did not seem to hear him. "Here of all places. Blood will tell, they say. Blood will tell. She came here out of the mountains, out of darkness to this place, and so this is where you came too. Even without knowing, you came here. And evil comes of it again." His eyes were wide and he was blinking very fast, looking at nothing.

Suspicion of his meaning began to creep into Bran's mind like an evening mist over the valley. "*Here.* You keep saying, *here* . . ."

"This was my house," Owen Davies said.

"No," Bran said. "Oh, no."

"Eleven years ago," Davies said, "I lived here."

"I didn't know. I never thought. It's been empty ever since I remember; I never thought of it being a proper house. I come here quite often when I'm out on my own. If it rains. Or just to sit. Sometimes" — he swallowed — "sometimes I pretend it's my house."

"It belongs to Caradog Prichard," his father said emptily. "His father kept it as the shepherd's house. But Prichard's men live by the farm now."

"I didn't realize," Bran said again.

Owen Davies stood over Pen, looking down, his thin shoulders bowed. He said bitterly, "The power of the Brenin Llwyd, aye. And that was what brought her out of the mountains to me, and then took her away again. Nothing else could have done it. I have tried to bring you up right, away from it all, in prayer and in goodness, and all the time the Brenin Llwyd has been reaching out to have you back where your mother went. You should not have come here."

"But I didn't know," Bran said. Anger flared in him suddenly like a blown spark. "How was I to know? You never told me. There's never anywhere else to go anyway. You don't let me go to Tywyn ever, not even to the pool or the beach after school with the others. Where else do you let me go except out on the moors? And how was I to know I shouldn't have come here?"

Davies said wretchedly, "I wanted to keep you free of it. It was over, it was gone, I wanted to keep you away from the past. Ah, we should never have stayed here. I should have moved away from the valley at the beginning."

Bran shook his head from side to side as if trying to cast something away from it; the air in the cottage seemed to be growing oppressive, heavy, filled with prickling tension like the forewarning of a thunderstorm. He said coldly, "You've never told me anything, ever. I just have to do what I am told all the time. *This is right, Bran, do it, this is for the best, this is the way you must behave.* You won't ever talk about my mam, you never have. I haven't got a mother — well, that's not so unusual, there's two boys at school haven't either. But I don't even know anything about mine. Only that her name was Gwen. And I know she had black hair and blue eyes, but that's only because Mrs Rowlands told me so, not you. You wouldn't ever tell me anything, except that she ran away when I was a baby. I don't even know whether she's alive or dead."

Owen Davies said quietly, "Neither do I, boy."

"But I want to know what she was like!" The tension sang in Bran's head like an angry sea; he was shouting now. "I want to know! And you're scared to tell me, because it must have been your fault she ran away! It was your fault, I've always known it was. You kept her shut off from everybody the way you've always kept me, and that's why she ran away!"

"No," his father said. He began walking unhappily to and fro in the little room; he looked at Bran anxiously, warily as if he were a wild animal that might spring. Bran thought the wariness was that of fear; there was nothing else in his experience that he could imagine it to be.

Owen Davies said, stumbling over the words, "You are young, Bran. You have to understand, I have always tried to do what is right, to tell you as much as is right. Not to tell you anything that might be dangerous for you —"

"Dangerous!" Bran said contemptuously. "How could it be dangerous to know about my mother?"

For a moment Davies's control cracked. "Look over there!" he snapped, pointing at Pen. The dog still lay motionless, dreadfully flattened down, like a skin pegged out to dry. "Look at that! You say that is the work of the Brenin Llwyd — and then you ask how there could be danger?"

"My mother has nothing to do with the Brenin Llwyd!" But as he heard his own words Bran stopped, staring.

His father said bleakly into the silence, "That is something we shall never know."

"What do you mean?"

"Listen. I do not know where she went. Out of the mountains she came, and back into the mountains she went, in the end, and none of us saw her again, ever." Owen Davies was forcing the words out one by one, with difficulty, as if each one gave him pain. "She went of her own choice, she ran away, and none knew why. I did not drive her away." His voice cracked suddenly. "Drive her away! *Iesu Crist*, boy. I was out of my head up in those hills looking for her, looking for her and never finding, calling, and never a word in return. And no sound anywhere but the birds crying, and the sheep, and the wind an empty whine in my ears. And the Brenin Llwyd behind his mist over Cader and Llyn Mwyngil, listening to the echo of my voice calling, smiling to himself that I never should know where she had gone . . ."

The anguish in his voice was so clear and unashamed that Bran fell silent, unable to break in.

Owen Davies looked at him. He said quietly, "I suppose it is time to tell you, since we have started this. I have had to wait, you see, until you were old enough to begin to understand. I am your legal father, Bran, because I adopted you right at the beginning. I have had you from when you were a baby, and God knows I am your father in my heart and soul. But you were not born to me and your mother. I cannot tell you who your real father was, she never said a word about him. When she came out of the mountains, out of nowhere, she brought you with her. She stayed with me for three days, and then she went away forever. And took a part of me with her." His voice shook, then steadied. "She left me a note."

He took his battered leather wallet out of his pocket and drew from an inner flap a small piece of paper. Unfolding it with great gentleness, he handed it to Bran. The paper was creased and fragile, almost parting at the folds; it bore only a few pencilled words, in a strangely rounded hand. *His name is Bran. Thank you, Owen Davies.*

Bran folded the note again, very slowly and carefully, and handed it back.

"It was all she left me of herself, Bran," said his father. "That note — and you."

Bran could think of no words to say. His head was crowded with jarring images and questions: a crossroads with a dozen turnings and no sign of which to follow. He thought, as he had thought a thousand times since he was old enough, of the enigma that was his mother, faceless, voiceless, her place in his life nothing but an aching absence. Now, across the years, she had brought him another absence, another emptiness: it was as if she were trying to take away his father as well — at any rate the father who, whatever their differences, he had always thought of as his own. Resentment and confusion rose and fell in Bran's mind like the wind. He thought wildly: *Who am I?* He looked at Pen, and the cottage, and the warestone of the Brenin Llwyd. He heard again his father's bitter remembering: *the Brenin Llwyd behind his mist over Cader and Llyn Mwyngil* . . . The names re-echoed round his head, and he could not understand why they should. Llyn Mwyngil, Tal y Llyn . . . the roaring in his head grew; it seemed to come from the warestone. He looked towards the stone. And again, as when Will had been there, the cottage seemed to grow dark, and the point of blue light began to shine out of the dim corner, and suddenly Bran had a strange jolting awareness of a part of his mind he had never been conscious of before. It was as if a door were opening somewhere within him, and he did not know what he would find on the other side. Flashing through his consciousness came a quick array of images, making no sense, like a dream dreamed while waking.

He thought he saw mist swirling on the mountain, and in it the tall blue-cloaked figure of the lord Will called Merriman, hooded, his head bent and his arm outstretched pointing down into a valley at a cottage — the cottage in which Bran now stood. For a flash Bran saw a woman, with black hair blowing, and he felt washed by love and tenderness, so that in longing he almost cried out to keep the feeling from flickering away. But then it was gone, and the mist swirled, and then again the hooded figure was there, and the woman too, looking back at the cottage, stretching out her arms in yearning. Then the figure of the lord called Merriman swept

199

his robed arm around the woman and they were both gone, vanished into the mist, out of sight and, he knew, out of the world. He saw only one other image: far below, through a break in the mist, the water of a distant lake glimmering like a lost jewel.

Bran did not understand. He knew that somehow he was seeing something out of the past concerning his mother, but there was not enough. What had Merriman to do with her coming, with its beginning and its end? He blinked, and found he was staring at his father again. Davies's eyes were wide in concern; he was clutching Bran's arm, and calling his name.

And in the new part of his mind that he had not seen before, Bran knew suddenly that he had now the power to do more things than he could ordinarily have done. He forgot all else that had happened that day, thinking only of the glimpse of his mother on a mountain over a glinting lake; all at once he wanted only to get to Tal y Llyn and the slopes of Cader Idris, to find out if this new part of his mind could sense there some further memory of the way he had begun. And he knew he could do something else, too. Leaping up, he called to the dog in a strong voice that seemed hardly his own, "*Tyrd yma*, Pen!"

And out of his flat-pressed paralysis the black sheepdog instantly rose, and leapt, and the boy and the dog ran out and away across the moor.

Owen Davies, his face lined old in fear and concern, stood silently watching for a moment.

Then he moved heavily out to the car, and drove out away from the cottage along the road to Idris Jones's farm.

Will rode more slowly than he had expected. The awkward shape of the harp, pressed against his chest, cut into his bruised arm and hurt so much that soon he could scarcely keep from dropping it. He stopped often to change its position. There were other reasons for pausing too, for the ferocity of malevolence building up in the valley now thrust at him like a great hand, pushing him away, threatening to clutch him in the giant fingers and crush him into nothingness. Doggedly Will rode on. First the cottage, then the lake. In the discordant chaos trying to force him back, only the simplest thoughts and images could survive, keep their shape. *First the cottage, then the lake.* He found himself saying it under his breath. Those were the two tasks for the harp that, above all else, he must make sure were carried out in these next two or three hours. The enchanted music must release Pen from the grip of the warestone, in the cottage, so that he would escape Caradog Prichard's gun. That was a simple matter. But then, more important than anything in the world, the music must wake the Sleepers of the pleasant lake, the creatures who slept their timeless sleep beside Tal y Llyn — whoever, and whatever, those creatures might be. For if a Lord of the Dark such as the Grey King could gain so astonishing a power as that now filling this valley, after centuries of murmuring sleep beneath his mountain, then indeed the Dark was rising, and its whole power increasing like a vast cloud threatening to engulf the whole world.

At last he came to the cottage. And found it empty.

Will stood in the bare stone-walled room, baffled and anxious. How could Pen have escaped the power of the warestone? Where was Bran? Had Caradog Prichard come hunting, with aid from the Grey King, and carried them both off? Impossible. Caradog Prichard was an unwitting servant, knowing nothing of his own links with the Grey King; he was a man only, with the instincts of a man — the worst instincts, with the best sadly submerged. *Where was Bran?*

He crossed to the corner of the room. The small white pebble that was the warestone lay just as it had lain before, innocuous and deadly. All around him the force of the Grey King's will beat implacably. *Go away, give up, you will not win, give up, go away.* Will cast desperately about through the powers of his own mind to find out what might have happened to Bran and the dog, but found nothing. He thought miserably: you should never have left them here alone. In a kind of angry self-abasement he leaned down once more and put his hand to the small round stone that he knew would be bound fast to the earth, beyond any ability of his to move it a fraction of an inch.

And the warestone came away as easily as any other stone, and lay loose in his palm, as if asking to be used.

Will stared at it. He could not believe what he saw. What had loosed the grip of the warestone? No magic he knew could do such a thing. It was a part of the Law, that the Light could not budge a warestone of the Dark, nor the Dark influence a warestone of the Light. That monstrous rigidity, once in force, could not be shattered by any but the stone's owner. Who then could have broken the power of the warestone of the Brenin Llwyd, other than the Brenin Llwyd himself, the Grey King?

Will shook his head impatiently. He was wasting time. One thing was certain, at any rate: left now without ownership, its control broken, the warestone was outside the Law and could itself be employed to tell him what had happened to bring it to its strange present state.

Will kept close hold of the harp; he felt he would never put it down again, least of all in this place. But he stood in the centre of the room with the warestone lying in his open palm, and he said certain words in the Old Speech, and emptied his mind and waited to receive whatever kind of awareness the stone could put into it. The knowledge would not be simple and open, he knew. It never was.

It came, as he stood there with his eyes closed and his mind thrumming, in a series of images so rapid that they were like a narrative, a piece of a story. Will saw a man's face, strong and handsome, but worn, with clear blue eyes and a grey beard. Though the clothes were strange and rich, he knew who it was in an instant: the face was that of the second lord in the cavern of Bird Rock, the Lord in the Sea-blue robe, who had spoken with such particular — and then unaccountable — closeness to Bran.

There was a deep sadness in the man's eyes. Will saw then the face of a woman, black-haired and blue-eyed, twisted in a dreadful mingling of grief and guilt. And somewhere with them he saw Merriman. Then he was seeing a different place, a low building with heavy stone walls and a cross above its roof — a church, or an abbey — and from it Merriman was leading the same woman, with a baby in her arms. They stood in a high place, on one of the Old Ways; there was a great whirling of mist; a rushing, and a flurry of images so fast that Will could not follow, nor make out more than a flash of the cottage, and an upright smiling Owen Davies with a younger, unlined face; and dogs and sheep and the mountain slopes green with bracken, and a voice calling, "Gwennie, Gwennie . . ."

Then, clearer than any, he saw Merriman, hooded in the dark blue robe, standing with the black-haired woman up on the slope above the Dysynni Valley, on Cadfan's Way. She was weeping quietly, tears running slow and glinting down her cheeks. She held nothing in her arms now. Merriman stretched out his hand, fingers stiff-straight, and Will heard through the whistle of the wind a thread of bell-like music that, as an Old One following the ways of the Old Ones, he had heard before in other places and times. Then the whirling came again, and all was confusion, though now he knew from the music that what he was witnessing was a travelling back to another age, long ago: the movement through Time that held no difficulty for an Old One, or a Lord of the Dark, though impossible for men except in dreams. In a last flashing image he saw the woman who had been with Merriman turn and go sadly back into the stone-built abbey, and disappear behind its heavy walls. And away alone elsewhere, yet superimposed on the abbey like the reflection in the glass that covers a picture, he saw the bearded face of the lord who had worn the sea-blue robe, with the gold circlet of a king crowning his head.

And suddenly Will understood the true nature of Bran Davies, the child brought out of the past to grow up in the future, and he felt a terrible compassion for his friend, born to a fearsome destiny of which, as yet, he could have no clear idea at all. It was hard even to think about so astounding a depth of power and responsibility. He saw now that he, Will Stanton, last of the Old Ones, had been fated all along to aid and support Bran in time to come, just as Merriman had always been at the side of Bran's great father. The father who had not known of his son's existence, back when he had been born, and who only now, over the centuries, had as a Lord of the High Magic seen him for the first time

. . . It was clear enough now how the ownership of the warestone had been broken. Beside a figure of this rank, the power of the Grey King dwindled to insignificance. But — that was true only if Bran truly knew what he was doing. How much of his buried and infinitely powerful nature had really been released? How much had he seen, in the cottage; what images had spun into his own unsuspecting mind?

Clutching the harp, forgetting his hurt arm in his haste, Will ran out of the cottage, clambered on the bicycle and made off along the road to Tal y Llyn. Bran could have gone nowhere else. All roads now must lead to the lake, and to the Sleepers. For at stake was not only the quest of the golden harp, the Sleepers' waking, but a power of the High Magic that could, if still unrecognized and uncontrolled, destroy not only that quest but the Light as well.

The Waking

When Will came to Tal y Llyn, he knew he must try to keep out of sight. There was no way of telling where Caradog Prichard might be; whether he had gone to Idris Jones's farm, where he would have turned from there ... Will thought of going to the farm to check, keeping hidden round the bend in the lane in case the battered grey van might be there. Then he changed his mind. There was too little time. Clutching his bundle, he rode on past the top of the Ty-Bont lane, and came to the corner where the road curved round the lake.

Tal y Llyn lay before him, rippled by the wind that all day had sent chunky cumulus clouds scudding across the sky. Green with grass and brown with bracken, the mountains swept out and up from its shores at both sides; the dark lake filled the valley all the way to the far end, where mountains met in a great V to make the pass of Tal y Llyn. Will stared at the rippled water.

Fire on the mountain shall find the harp of gold
Played to wake the Sleepers, oldest of the old ...

Where should it be played, and when? Not here, out on the unprotected valley road . . . He turned left and rode towards the side of the valley where, above the low gentle green fields, the first dark slopes of Cader Idris climbed like a wall roofed by the sky. It was the slope on which they had found the dead sheep; the slope that its master the Grey King had shaken to throw Will down into the lake. Yet the instinct of the Old Ones drove Will to struggle towards it; to make for the stronghold of the enemy, in a deliberate challenge to the furious force driving him back. The greater the odds, he thought, the greater the victory.

There was a muted roaring in his ears, as he rode on with the bundled harp beneath his arm. Nearer and nearer the mountainside loomed above him. Soon the road would curve away. To stay by the lake, he must dismount and climb over the fields and up the slope of treacherous loose scree, to stand isolated overlooking the water. But he felt that was where he must go.

Then swiftly, suddenly, Caradog Prichard stepped into the road in front of him and grabbed the handlebars of the bike, so that Will tumbled sideways into a painful heap on the ground.

As he scrambled up, clutching the harp with an arm now hurting still more, Will felt not anger or fear but acute irritation. Prichard: always Prichard! While the Grey King loomed in dire threat over the Light, Prichard like a squealing mouse must endlessly intrude to tug Will down to the petty rivalries and rages of ordinary men. He glared at Caradog Prichard with a mute disdain that the man had not the wit to recognize as being dangerous.

"Where you going, English?" said Prichard, holding the bicycle firmly. His thinning red hair was dishevelled; his small eyes glittered oddly.

Will said, cold as winter fish, "That has nothing whatsoever to do with you."

"Manners, manners," said Caradog Prichard. "I know very well where you are going, my sweet young man — you and Bran Davies are trying to hide that other damn sheep-killing dog. But there is not a single way in the world that you are going to keep me from him. What you got there, then, eh?"

In mindless suspicion he reached for the sacking-swathed bundle beneath Will's arm.

Will's reaction was quicker even than his own eye could follow. The harp was far, far too important to be placed in such foolish jeopardy. Instantly, he was an Old One in the full blaze of power, rearing up terrible as a pillar of light. Towering in fury, he stretched an arm pointing at Caradog Prichard — but met, in answering rage, a barrier of furious resistance from the Grey King.

At first Prichard cringed before him, his eyes wide and his mouth slack with terror, expecting annihilation. But as he found himself protected, slowly craftiness woke in his eyes. Will watched warily, knowing that the Brenin Llwyd was taking the greatest of all risks that any lord of the Light or the Dark could take, by channelling his own immense power through an ordinary mortal who had not the slightest awareness of the appalling forces at his command. The Lord of the Dark must be in a desperate state, to trust his cause to so perilous a servant.

"Leave me alone, Mr Prichard," Will said. "I have not got John Rowlands's dog with me. I don't even know where he is."

"Oh, yes, you do know, boy, and so do I." The words tumbled out of Prichard, nearer the surface of his mind than the wonder at his new gift. "He has been taken to Jones Ty-Bont's farm, to be kept from me so that he can get back to his murderous business again. But it will not work, indeed no, no hope of it, I am not such a fool." He glared at Will. "And you had better tell me where he is, boy, tell me what you are all up to, or it will go very badly with you."

Will could sense the man's anger and malice whirling round his mind like a maddened bird caught in a room without exit. *Ah, Brenin Llwyd*, he thought with a kind of sadness, *your powers deserve better than to be put into one without discipline or training, without the wit to use them properly . . .*

He said, "Mr Prichard, please leave me alone. You don't know what you are doing. Really. I don't want to have to hurt you."

Caradog Prichard stared at him for a moment of genuine blank wonder, like a man in the instant before he understands the point of a joke, and then he broke into gulping laughter. "You don't want to hurt me? Well, that's very nice, now, I am delighted to hear it, very thoughtful. Very kind . . ."

The sunshine that had intermittently lit the morning was gone now; grey cloud was thickening over the sky, sweeping down the valley on the wind that rippled the lake. Some instinct at the back of Will's mind made him suddenly aware of the grey-ness growing like a weight all around, and woke the decision that took hold of him as Caradog Prichard's jeering laughter spluttered down into control. He took a step or two backwards, holding the harp close at his side. Then half closing his eyes, he called silently to the gifts that had made him an Old One in full strength, to the spells that made him able to ride the wind, to fly beyond the sky and beneath the sea; to the circle of the Light that had set him on this quest for the last link in their defence against the Dark's rising.

There was a sound like the murmuring sea out of the still lake Tal y Llyn, Llyn Mwyngil, and from the far edge of the dark water a huge wave came travelling. It curled up high and white-topped, fringed with foam as if about to break. Yet it did not break, but swept on across the water towards them, and on its curving peak rode six white swans, moving smooth as glass, their great wings out-stretched and touching wing-tip to wing-tip. They were enormous, powerful birds, their white feathers shining like polished silver even in the grey light

211

of the cloud-hung sky. As they drew nearer and nearer, one of the swans raised its head on the curving, graceful neck and gave a long mournful cry, like a warning, or a lament.

On and on they came, towards the shore, towards Will and Caradog Prichard. The wave loomed higher and higher: a green wave, glowing with a strange translucent light that seemed to come out of the bottom of the lake. It was clear that the birds would dive upon them, and the wave break over them and rush forward down the valley, with all the water of the lake in one long rush, sweeping farms and houses and people before it in total devastation, down to the sea.

Will knew this not to be true, but it was the image that he was forcing into Caradog Prichard's mind.

The white swan gave one more whooping, mourning cry, the shriek of a soul in utter emptiness, and Caradog Prichard stumbled backwards, his small eyes bulging in his head from horror and disbelief, one hand clutched in his red hair. He opened his mouth, and strange wordless sounds came out of it. Then something seemed to seize him, and he jerked into a frozen immobility, arms and legs caught at unnatural angles; and the air was filled with a rushing, hissing sound that came so quickly its direction could not be told.

But Will, appalled, knew what it must be. By accepting help from the Dark, the Welshman had doomed his own mind.

212

He saw in Caradog Prichard's eyes the quick flash of madness as human reason was swept aside by the dreadful power of the Grey King. He saw the mind sway as the body was, still unwittingly, possessed. Prichard's back straightened; his pudgy form seemed to rise taller than before, and the shoulders hunched themselves in a hint of immense strength. The force of the Brenin Llwyd's magic was in him and pulsing out of him, and he stared at the advancing wave and shrieked in a cracked voice some words of Welsh.

And the swans rose crying into the air and curved away on long slow-beating wings, for all at once the rearing wave collapsed, dragged down into heaviness by a tremendous churning and heaving of thousand upon thousand fish. Silver and grey and dark glinting green they boiled on the surface, perch and trout and wriggling eels, and slant-mouthed pike with needle teeth and small evil eyes. It was as if all the fish in all the lakes of Wales seethed there in a huge mass on the water of Llyn Mwyngil, smoothing its surface into a quivering stillness. Yet it was with the use of a voice and a mind no more than human that so great a spell had been cast. A chill struck into Will as he understood this new deviousness of the Brenin Llwyd. There would be no open confrontation. He himself would never see the Grey King again, for in such a facing of two poles of enchantment there was danger of annihilation for one. Instead Will would face, as he was facing now, the power of the Grey King channelled through the mind of an evil-wishing but innocent man: a man made into a dreadfully vulnerable vessel for the Dark. If the Light were to give any final annihilating stroke in this encounter, the Dark would still be protected, but the mind of the man would inevitably be destroyed. Caradog Prichard, if he were still sane now, would be driven then forever into hopeless madness. Unless Will could somehow avoid such an encounter, there was no help for it. The Grey King was using Prichard as a shield, knowing that he himself could remain protected if the shield were destroyed.

Will called out in anguish, hardly knowing he did so, "Caradog Prichard! Stop! Leave us alone! For your own sake, leave me alone!"

But there was nothing he could do. The momentum of their conflict was already too great, like a wheel spinning faster and faster downhill. Caradog Prichard was gazing in childish delight at the lake of seething fish, rubbing his hands together, talking steadily to himself in Welsh. He looked at Will and giggled. He did not stop talking, but switched to English, the words coming out in a half-crazed conversational stream, very fast.

"You see the pretty creatures now, so many thousands of them, and all ours and doing what we ask, more of a match for six swans than you were expecting, eh, *dewinn bach*? Ah, you do not know what you are up against, enough nonsense we have had now, my friends and me, it is time that you are going to show me the dog, the dog, because anything

214

you do to try and turn us aside will be no use at all.
No use at all. So I want the dog now, English, you
are to tell me where I can find the dog, and my
good gun is there in the car waiting for him and
there will be no more sheep-killing in this valley. I
shall see to that."

He was watching Will, the little eyes darting up
and down like small fish themselves, and suddenly
once more his gaze fastened on the sacking-bundled
harp.

"But first I would like to know what that really
is under your arm there, boy, so I think you will
show me that if you would like us to leave you
alone." He giggled again on the last word, and Will
knew that there was no hope now of reaching the
side of the mountain, the place from which it would
have been safest and most fitting to play the golden
harp. He stepped slowly backwards, in a smooth
movement designed to keep Caradog Prichard from
alarm, and as caution woke too late in the farmer's
bright eyes, he slipped the harp out from its
covering, laid it crooked in one arm as he had seen
Bran do, and swept the fingers of the other hand
over its strings.

And so the world changed.

Already now the sky was a heavier grey than it
had been, as the afternoon darkened towards
evening and the clouds thickened for rain. But as
the lilting flow of notes from the little harp poured
out into the air, in an aching sweetness, a strange
glow seemed very subtly to begin shining out of

lake and cloud and sky, mountain and valley, bracken and grass. Colours grew brighter, dark places more intense and secret; every sight and feeling was more vivid and pronounced. The fish covering the whole swaying surface of the lake began to change; flickering silver, fish after fish leapt into the air and curved down again, until the lake seemed no longer burdened with a great weight of sluggish creatures, but alive and dancing with bright streaks of silver light.

And out of the sky at the seaward end of the valley, down towards the lake, another sound rose over the sweet arpeggios lilting to and fro as Will ran his fingers gently up and down the strings of his harp. There was a harsh crying, like the calling of seagulls. And flying in groups and pairs, without formation, came swooping the strange ellipsoid black forms of cormorants, twenty or thirty of them, more than Will had ever seen flying together. The kings of the bird-fishermen of the sea, never normally seen away from the sea and its cliffs and crags, they came skimming down to the surface of Llyn Mwyngil and began snatching up the leaping fish, and Will remembered suddenly Bran's stories of how the Bird Rock, Craig yr Aderyn, is the only place in the world where cormorants are known to gather and build their nests inland, because in the land of the Grey King the coast has no rocky cliffs for such building, but only sand and beaches and dunes.

216

Down they swept. The fish jumped, sparkling; the cormorants gulped them; swerved away; dived and gulped again. Caradog Prichard gave a cross wail like a disappointed child. The curious light glimmered through the valley. Still Will's fingers flickered over the harp, and the music rippled out deliberate and clear as spring water. He was caught up in a tension that prickled through him like electricity, a fierce anticipation of unknown wonders; he felt as taut as though every hair stood on end. And then, all at once, the fish vanished, the surface of the lake was suddenly smooth as dark glass, and all the cormorants swept upwards in a cloud and curved away, shrieking, disappearing back up the long broad valley to Bird Rock. And through the luminescence that held the valley suspended in daylit, moonlit half-light, Will saw six figures take shape.

They were horsemen, riding. They came out of the mountain, out of the lowest slopes of Cader Idris that reached up from the lake into the fortresses of the Grey King. They were silvery-grey, glinting figures riding horses of the same strange half-colour, and they rode over the lake without touching the water, without making any sound. The music of the harp lapped them round, and as they drew near, Will saw that they were smiling. They wore tunics and cloaks. Each one had a sword hanging at his side. Two were hooded. One wore a circlet about his head, a gleaming circlet of nobility, though not the crown of a king. He turned to Will, as the

217

ghostly group rode by, and bent his smiling bearded head in greeting. The music rippled bell-like round the valley from the harp in Will's hands, and Will bent his own head in sober greeting but did not break his playing.

The riders rode past Caradog Prichard, who stood gaping vacantly at the lake, looking for the vanished wondrous fish, and clearly did not see anything else. *He has the power of the Grey King*, Will thought, *but not the eyes* . . . Then the riders wheeled back suddenly towards the slope of the mountain, and before Will could wonder at it, he saw that Bran stood there on the slope, halfway up the loose scree, near the ledge that had broken his own fall earlier that day. The black sheepdog Pen was beside him, and toiling up the slope after them was Owen Davies, bent and weary, with the same blankness in his face that Caradog Prichard wore. It was not for ordinary men to see that the Sleepers, woken out of their long centuries of rest, were riding now to the rescue of the world from the rising Dark.

But Bran could see.

He stood watching the Sleepers with a blaze of delight in his pale face. He raised one hand to Will, and opened both arms in a gesture of admiration at the playing of the harp. For a moment he seemed no more than an uncomplicated small boy, caught up in bubbling wonder by a marvellous sight. But only for a moment. The six riders, glinting silver-grey on their silver-grey mounts, curved round after their leader and paused for a moment in line before the place on the hillside where Bran stood. Each drew his sword and held it upright before his face in a salute, and kissed the flat of its blade in homage as to a king. And Bran stood there slim and erect as a young tree, his white hair gleaming in a silver crest, and bent his head gravely to them with the quiet arrogance of a king granting a boon.

Then they sheathed their swords again and wheeled about, and the silver-grey horses sprang up into the sky. And the Sleepers, wakened and riding, rose high over the lake and away, disappearing further and further into the gathering gloom of the Tal y Llyn pass and beyond, until they were gone from the valley, and beyond, and could be seen no more.

Will stilled his fingers on the golden harp, and its delicate melody died, leaving only the whisper of the wind. He felt drained, as though all strength had gone out of him. For the first time he remembered that he was not only an Old One, but also a convalescent, still weak from the long illness that in the beginning had sent him to Wales.

For a flicker of an instant too, then, he remembered what John Rowlands had said about the coldness at the heart of the Light, as he realized by what agency he must have become so suddenly and severely ill. But it was only for an instant. To an Old One such things were not of importance.

All at once he was brushed aside, and a hasty rough hand snatched the golden harp from his grasp. The power of the Grey King seemed gone from Caradog Prichard, but he was not what he had been before it had come.

"So that is what it's all about, then," Prichard said thickly. "A bloody harp, a little gold thing just like she was playing."

"Give it back," Will said. Then he paused. "*She?*"

"It is a Welsh harp, English, an old one." Prichard peered owlishly at it. "What might it be doing in your hands? You have no right to be holding a Welsh harp." Suddenly he was glaring viciously at Will. "Go home. Go back where you belong. Mind your business."

Will said, "The harp has fulfilled its purpose. What did you mean, *like she was playing?*"

"Mind your business," Prichard said again, savagely. "A long time ago, and nothing to do with you."

From the corner of his eye Will could see that Owen Davies had joined Bran up on the hillside, with Pen darting restlessly between them. Desperately he tried to will Bran to move away, out of sight; he could not understand why he stayed there in the open, where a casual glance would show them to Caradog Prichard. *Move!* he shouted silently. *Go away!* But it was too late. Something, perhaps the sheepdog's anxious wheeling, had caught Prichard's eye; he glanced half-consciously up at the mountain, and he froze.

Every part of the moment seared itself into Will's brain, so that ever afterwards he could feel the quick roaring of impending disaster and see like a bright

220

picture the heavy grey sky, the rearing mountain, the rippling dark lake, the startling patches of colour made by a white-haired boy and a man with flaring red hair: and over it all the strange glow of a light like the warning luminousness hanging over a countryside before a dreadful storm. Caradog Prichard turned towards him a face marked with a terrible mingling of anger, reproach, and pain, and at the heart of them all a thin core of hatred and the urge to hurt back. Looking deliberately into Will's face, he heaved back his arm and flung the golden harp far out into the lake. Ripples circled outward on the dark water, and then were still.

Then Prichard ran, light as a boy, throwing himself forward to the mountain, and to Bran standing there like a figurehead with the dog Pen. At the last moment before the slope he turned aside, along the curving road that led back down the valley; and Will saw that he had left the small grey van there in the road and was running towards it now with desperate speed.

In the same moment he realized why, and flung a great spell of prevention at Prichard — only to have it cast aside by the protection of the Grey King that the farmer, unknowing, still carried with him. Caradog Prichard reached the van, snatched open its back doors and brought out his long-muzzled shotgun, the same gun with which he had shot Bran's dog Cafall. Swiftly he cocked the gun, swung round and began walking, deliberately and steadily, towards the boy and the dog on the hill. He had no need for haste now. There was no cover to which they could run. Will dug his fingernails into his palms, his mind thrashing for an effective defence. Then he heard the sound of a noisy car.

The Land-Rover swung at astonishing speed out of the lane from Ty-Bont Farm, and round the corner to the lake. John Rowlands must have seen Prichard and his van and his gun all in one appalled moment, for the chunky little car rushed forward to a jerking halt almost at the farmer's feet. The door seemed hardly open before John Rowlands's lanky form was out. He stood still, facing Caradog Prichard and the boy and the dog on the hillside beyond. "Caradog," he said. "There is no sheep here with its throat cut. You have no right, and no need."

Prichard's voice was high and dangerous. "There is a sheep dead up there now!" And Will saw that the body of the ewe attacked by the *milgwn*, still up there on its ledge, was visible as a white heap from where they stood. He knew then for the first time why the Grey King had made sure that his *milgwn* should bring it to that spot.

"That is a Pentref sheep, from those wintering at Clwyd," John Rowlands said.

"Oh, very likely," said Prichard, sneering.

"I will show you. Come up and see."

"Even if it were, what of that? It is still that murdering dog of yours that does these things — to sheep in your own care too, is it? What is the matter with you, Rowlands, that you keep him?"

His face glistening with the sweat of rage, Prichard brought up his gun level with his waist, facing the hill.

"*No*," John Rowlands said behind him, his voice very deep.

Something in Caradog Prichard cracked, and he swung round to face Rowlands, the gun still pointing. His voice pitched itself higher still, he was like a wire about to break.

"Always pushing your nose in, you are, John Rowlands. Trying to stop me now, the way you stopped me before. You should not have stopped me then, I would have fought him harder and won, and then she would have come with me. She would have come with me, if it had not been for you pushing in."

His hands were white where they clenched the gun; his words came out so fast they fell over themselves. John Rowlands stood speechless, staring at him, and Will saw understanding gradually follow astonishment on the tough kind face as he realized what Prichard was talking about.

But before he could speak, Owen Davies's voice came unexpectedly strong and clear from the hillside above them, like a bell ringing out. "Oh, no, indeed, she would not have come with you, Caradog. Never. And you were not winning that fight and you would never have won in a hundred years, and it was lucky for you that John Rowlands did break into it. I did not know what I was doing, but I would have killed you if I could, for hurting my Gwen."

"Your Gwen?" Prichard spat the words at him. "Any man's Gwen! That was as clear as the light in the sky. Why else would she choose a man like you, Owen Davies? A lovely wild thing out of the mountains she was, with a face like a flower, and fingers that made music out of that little harp that she carried like no music you ever heard before . . ." For an instant there was a terrible yearning in his voice. But almost as soon again, the tortured, half-crazed face twisted back into malevolence. He looked at Bran's white head.

"And the bastard son there, that you kept all these years to torment me, to remind me — you had no right to him either, I could have looked after her and her child better than you —"

Bran said in a high remote voice, that seemed to come so far out of the past that it put a chill into Will's spine: "And would you then have shot my dog Cafall, Mr Prichard?"

"Not even your own dog, that animal was not," Prichard said roughly. "That was a working dog of your father's."

"Oh, yes," said Bran in the same clear distant voice. "Yes, indeed. My father had a dog named Cafall."

Will's blood tingled in his veins, for he knew that the Cafall of whom Bran spoke was not the dog Cafall who had been shot, and the father not Owen Davies. So now Bran, the Pendragon, must know of his true, magnificent, dreadful heritage. Then a last sudden astonishment woke in Will's mind. It must have been Owen Davies who gave the dead dog his name, for Bran had said that Cafall had come to them when he himself was only a very small boy. *Why had Owen Davies named his son's dog by the name of the great king's hound?*

His eyes flickered to Owen Davies's thin unprepossessing form, and he saw that the man was watching him.

"Oh, yes," Davies said. "I knew. I tried not to believe it, but I've always known. She came from Cader Idris, you see, and that is the Seat of Arthur, in English. With Arthur's son she came out of the past, because she had betrayed the king her lord and was afraid that he would cast out his own son as a result. By enchantment of the *dewin* she brought the boy into the future, away from their troubles — the future that is the present time now for us. And she left him here. And perhaps, perhaps, she would not herself have had to go back into the past, if the fat fool there had not interfered, and heard the harp, and wanted my Guinevere, and tried to take her away."

He looked coldly down at Caradog Prichard. With a snarl of fury Prichard jerked his gun up to his shoulder, but John Rowlands swiftly reached out a long arm and wrenched it from him before his finger could reach the trigger. Prichard shouted angrily, gave him a great push and leapt away, scrambling up in venomous fury towards the ledge where Bran and Owen Davies stood.

Bran went to Davies and put his arm round his waist, and stood close. It was the first gesture of affection between the two that Will had ever seen. And wondering, loving surprise woke in Owen Davies's worn face as he looked down at the boy's white head, and the two stood there, waiting.

Prichard scrambled towards them, murder in his eyes. But John Rowlands was close behind him. He swung the gun at Prichard like a stick, knocking him sideways, and then seized and held him with the force of a much younger man. Wildly struggling, but grasped into helplessness, Caradog Prichard put back his head and gave a terrible shriek of madness, as all control from the Dark left him, and his mind collapsed into the wreck it must now remain. And with the Sleepers ridden, and the last hope of harming Bran gone, the Grey King gave up his battle.

The echoes of Prichard's shriek became a long howling cry through the mountains, rising, falling, rising, echoing from peak to peak, as all powers of the Dark vanished forever from Cader Idris, from the valley of the Dysynni, from Tal y Llyn. Cold as death, anguished as all the loss in the world, it died away and yet still seemed to hang in the air.

They stood motionless, caught in horror.

And the mist that men called the breath of the Grey King came creeping down out of the pass and down the side of the mountains, rolling and curling and wisping, concealing all it reached, until at the last it cut off every one of them from the rest. A rustling, flurrying sound came out of the mist, but only Will saw the great grey forms of the ghost foxes, the *milgwn* of the Brenin Llwyd, come rushing headlong down the mountain, and plunge into the dark lake, and disappear.

Then the mist closed over Llyn Mwyngil, the lake in the pleasant retreat, and there was a cold silence through all the valley save for the distant bleat, sometimes, of a mountain sheep, like the echo of a man's voice calling a girl's name, far away.